FALCO

He woke up
roundings, g
an old, old r   a slim sexless
figure hidden completely under long blue
veils.

These two called him Adric, a name he instinctively responded to, even though he knew he was Mike Kenscott, radio engineer in a government laboratory. His rich crimson clothing was unfamiliar and he was shocked by the landscape he saw through the window—mountains bathed in a pinkish light whose source was not one but two brilliant suns.

Panic seized him then. Who were these people? What world was he in? And, most important, whom had he become?

Also in Legend by Marion Zimmer Bradley

THE DARKOVER NOVELS:

Darkover Landfall
Hawkmistress!
The Shattered Chain
Thendara House
City of Sorcery
Winds of Darkover
Spell Sword
The Forbidden Tower
The Bloody Sun
Heritage of Hastur
Sharra's Exile
The World Wreckers

FALCONS OF NARABEDLA

Marion Zimmer Bradley

A Legend book published by
Arrow Books Limited
62–65 Chandos Place, London WC2N 4NW

An imprint of Century Hutchinson Limited

London Melbourne Sydney Auckland
Johannesburg and agencies throughout
the world

First published in 1964 by Ace Books, USA
First published in Great Britain by Arrow 1984
Legend edition 1988

© Ace Books Inc. 1964

This book is sold subject to the condition that it shall not, by way of trade or otherwise, be lent, re-sold, hired out, or otherwise circulated without the publisher's prior consent in any form of binding or cover other than that in which it is published and without a similar condition including this condition being imposed on the subsequent purchaser

Printed and bound in Great Britain by
Anchor Brendon Limited, Tiptree, Essex

ISBN 0 09 935650 3

FOREWORD

When I was about eight years old, in the attic of the somewhat Lovecraftian old farmhouse where I was brought up, I discovered a cardboard carton chock full and overflowing with old pulp magazines—*Argosy, Blue Book, Weird Tales,* and the like. I read them for hours, lying flat on my stomach in the dusty sunlight on the landing, the smell of plaster in my nostrils, a screechy old Victrola playing Caruso records above me; sometimes I'd get so absorbed in my story that the Victrola would run down, emitting weird noises until I scrambled up to wind it absent-mindedly with one arm.

In my late teens, I discovered the science-fiction pulps, and the way they mingled my beloved fantasies with science and adventure—the great names of Kuttner, Hamilton, Brackett. All too soon, spurred on by an era of scientific strides, adventure-fantasy vanished, to be superseded by the era of drab realism: the "sand-in-my spacesuit" school. I have nothing against meticulously constructed, realistic science-fiction. I even like to write it, sometimes. But I got nostalgic for the old days, the glint of strange suns on worlds that never were and never would be.

And it seems that I'm not the only one. Adventure fantasy, sword-and-sorcery—by whatever name, it's catching on all over again; perhaps in a slightly more sophisticated form, but it has basically the same appeal; the gleam and glow of a dark world, the flash of the wing of a falcon—like, perhaps, the falcons of Narabedla....

—M.Z.B.

CHAPTER ONE

SOMEWHERE on the crags above us, I heard a big bird scream.

I turned to Andy, knee-deep in the icy stream beside me. "There's your eagle. Probably smells that cougar I shot yesterday." I started to reel in my line, knowing what my brother's next move would be. "Get the camera, and we'll try for a picture."

We crouched together in the underbrush, watching, as the big bird of prey wheeled down in a slow spiral toward the dead cougar. Andy was trembling with excitement, the camera poised against his chest. "Golly," he whispered, almost prayerfully, "six-foot wing spread at least, maybe more—"

The bird screamed again, warily, head cocked into the wind. We were to leeward; the scent of the carrion masked our enemy smell from him. The eagle failed to scent or to see us, swooping down and dropping on the cougar's head. Andy's camera clicked twice. The eagle thrust in its beak.

A red-hot wire flared in my brain. The bird—the bird—I leaped out of cover, running swiftly across the ten-foot clearing that separated us from the attacking eagle, my hand tugging automatically at the hunting knife in my belt. Andy's shout of surprise and dismay was a far-away noise in my ears as the eagle started away with flapping, angry wings—then, in fury, swept down at me, pinions beating around my head. I heard and felt the wicked beak dart in, and thrust blindly upward with the knife: ripped, slashing, hearing the bird's scream of pain and the flapping of wide wings.

A red-hot haze spun around me—

This had happened before. I had fought like this before, for my life, for my life—

Then the screaming eagle was gone, a lifting cry down-wind and a vanishing shadow, and Andy's rough grip was on my shoulder, shaking me, hard. His voice, furious and frightened, was barely recognizable. "Mike! Mike, you damned idiot, are you all right? You must be crazy!"

I blinked, rubbing my hand across my eyes. The hand came away red. I was standing in the clearing, the knife in my hand red with blood. Bird blood. I heard myself ask, stupidly, "What happened?"

My brother's face came clear through the red haze, scowling wrathfully. "You tell *me* that! Mike, what in the devil were you thinking of? You told me yourself that an eagle will attack a man if it's bothered. I had him square in the camera when you jumped out of there like a bat out of a belfry, and went for the eagle with your knife. You must be clean crazy!"

I let the knife drop out of my hand. "Yeah," I said heavily, "I guess I spoiled your picture, Andy. I'm sorry. I didn't . . ." My voice trailed off, helpless. I felt like a prize fool. The kid's hand was still on my shoulder. He let it fall away and knelt in the grass, groping for his camera. "That's all right, Mike," he said in a dead voice. "You scared the daylights out of me, that's all."

He stood up swiftly, looking straight into my face.

"Only—damn it, Mike, you've been acting crazy for a week. I don't mind the blasted camera, but when you start going for eagles with your bare hands—" abruptly he flung the camera away, turned, and began to run down the slope in the direction of the cabin.

I took one step to follow, then stopped, bending to retrieve the broken pieces of Andy's cherished camera. He must have hit the eagle with it. Lucky thing for me. Even a hawk can be a mean bird, and an eagle—Why, why in the hell had I done a thing like that? I'd warned Andy, time and time again, to stay clear of the big birds.

Now that the urgency of action had deserted me, I felt stupid and a little light-headed. I didn't wonder that Andy thought I was crazy. I thought so myself, more than half the time. I stowed the broken camera in my tackle box, mentally promising Andy a better one, hunted up the abandoned lines and poles, cleaned our day's catch. It was dark before I started for the cabin; I could hear the hum of the electric dynamo I'd rigged, and see the electric light across the dusk of the Sierras. A smell of bacon greeted me as I crossed into the glare of the unshielded bulb. Andy hadn't waited for the fish. He was standing at the cookstove, his back stubbornly turned to me. He did not turn.

"Andy—" I said.

"It's okay, Mike. Sit down and eat your supper."

"Andy—I'll get you another camera."

"I said, it's okay. Now, damn it, eat."

He didn't speak again for some time; but as I stretched back for a second mug of coffee, he got up and began to walk restlessly around the room.

"Mike, you came here for a rest," he said at last. "Why can't you lay off your everlasting work for a while, and relax?" He looked disgustedly over his shoulder at the work table where the light spilled over a confused litter of wires and magnets and coils. "You're turning this place into a branch office of General Electric."

"I can't stop now," I said violently, "I'm on the track of something, maybe something big, and if I stop now, I'll never find it!"

"Must be real important," Andy said sourly, "if it makes you act like bughouse bait."

I shrugged, not answering. We'd been over that before. I'd known it when they threw me out of the government lab, just before the big blowup. I thought angrily, *Maybe I'm heading for another one.* But I didn't care.

"Sit down, Andy," I told him. "You don't know what happened down there. No, it's not any military secret, or anything. It was all declassified a long time before I finished my service hitch." I paused, swallowing down the coffee, not caring that it scalded my mouth. I said, with the old bitterness, "Except for me."

I'd been working in a government radio lab, on some new communications equipment. Since I'd never finished it, there's no point in going into details. It's enough to say that it would have made radar as obsolete as the stagecoach.

I'd built a special supersonic condenser, and had had trouble with a set of magnetic coils that wouldn't wind properly. When the thing blew up, I hadn't had any sleep for three nights, but that wasn't the reason. That was normal around there. *I* was normal then, just another communications man, a little bug-eyed about the kind of research tinkering I liked, but without any of the crazy impractical notions that had lost me my job afterward. They called it overwork. Only I know they thought the explosion had disturbed my brain. I didn't blame them. Sometimes I thought so myself. Or at least I'd have liked to think so.

It started one day in the lab with a shadow on the sun and an elusive short-circuit somewhere that kept giving me shock after shock until I was dizzy. By the time I got it fixed—and I never could figure out why *that* circuit should have shorted—the oscillator had gone out of control, or so I thought. I kept getting a series of low-frequency waves that were like nothing I'd ever seen before. Then there was something like a voice, speaking out of a very old, jerry-built crystal set —only there wasn't a radio receiver, or a speaker, anywhere in the lab, and nobody else heard it. I wasn't sure myself, because right then, every instrument in the place went haywire; and forty seconds later, part of the ceiling hit the floor, and the floor went up through the roof. They found me, they say, half-crushed under a beam. Anyway, I woke up in a hospital, with four cracked ribs, and feeling as if I'd had a lot of voltage poured into me.

It went down in the report that I'd been struck by lightning. They had to say something.

It took me a long time to get well. The ribs, and the other things, healed fast—faster than the doctors liked. I didn't mind the hospital part, except that I couldn't walk without shaking, or light a cigarette without burning myself, for weeks. The thing I minded was what I remembered from *before* I woke up.

Delirium. That was what they told me. But the kind and type of marks all over my body didn't ring true. Electricity—even freak lightning—doesn't make those kinds of burns. And this corner of the world doesn't make a habit of branding people.

Only before I could show the marks to anyone outside the hospital, they were gone. Not healed, just gone. I remember the look on the intern's face when I showed him the spots where the burns had been. He didn't think I was crazy. He thought *he* was.

There was a psychiatrist sniffing around, too, putting forth slow, soothing suggestions about psychosomatic medicine and hysterical stigmata, but that was just for the record, too.

I knew the lab hadn't been struck by lightning. The Major knew it, too. I found that out the day I reported back to work. All the time we talked, his big pen moved in stubby circles across the pages of his logbook, and he talked without raising his head to look at me.

"I know all that, Kenscott. No electrical storms reported in the vicinity, no radio disturbances within a thousand miles. But," his jaw was stubborn, "the lab was wrecked and you were hurt. We've got to have something for the record."

I could understand all that. What I resented was the way they treated me when I went back to work. They transferred me to another division and another project. They turned down my request to follow up research on those low-frequency waves. My private notes were ripped out of my notebook while I was at lunch, and I never saw them again. And as soon as they could, they shipped me to Fairbanks, Alaska, and that was the end of that.

The Major told me all I needed to know, the day before I took the plane to Alaska. His scowl said more than his words, and they said plenty.

"I'd let it alone, Kenscott. No sense stirring up more trouble. We can't monkey with side alleys, anyhow. Next time, you might get your head blown off, not just a dose of stray voltage out of the blue. We've done everything but stand on our heads, trying to find out where that spare energy came from and where it went."

"Then you admit there *was* something!" That was more than I'd been able to get from anyone else on the project.

"Unofficially, yes." The Major scowled, not looking at me. Then it all came out in a single fast string of words. "What it boils down to is that it shows up when you're around, and it *doesn't* show up when you're *not* around, and we don't know if it's fakery or poltergeists or ESP but we don't want any more of it, whatever it is. We've marked that whole line of research *closed*, Kenscott. And if I were you I'd call myself lucky and keep my mouth shut about it."

"It wasn't a message from Mars," I suggested without smiling, and he didn't think it was funny either. But there was relief on his face when I left the office and went to clean out my drawer.

I got along all right in Alaska, for a while. They put me on paperwork, routine supervisory jobs, and ignored me when I tried to get back to the practical end of it. And then they shipped me back to the States, with a discharge, and a recommendation of a long rest. I tried to explain it to Andy:

"They called it overwork. They said I needed rest.

Maybe so. The shock did something funny to me—tore me open—like the electric shock treatments they give catatonic patients. I seem to know a lot of things I never learned. Ordinary radio work doesn't seem to mean much to me any more. It doesn't make sense. And every now and then something will *start* to make sense, and then doesn't. When people out West were talking about Flying Saucers, whatever they were, and when there was all that talk about atomic fallout changing the weather, and the cloud-seeding experiments, all this sort of halfway made sense for a while. Only I kept expecting it to happen without"— I moved my hand, helplessly, trying to put words to a random impression—"without people having to go up there in planes and *do* anything about it. And when we came up here—" I paused, trying to fit more confused impressions together. He wasn't going to believe me anyhow, but I wanted him to. A tree slapped against the cabin window, and I jumped.

"It started the day we came into the mountains. Energy out of nowhere, following me around. It can't knock me out. Have you noticed that I let *you* turn the lights on and off? The day we came up here, I shorted my electric razor," I rubbed my hand over a stubbled face, "and I blew out five fuses trying to change one. Remember?"

"Yeah, I remember: we had to drive into town for some more." My brother's eyes rested uneasily on my face. "Mike, listen—you *are* kidding, aren't you?"

"I wish I were," I said. "That energy just drains into me and nothing happens. I'm immune." I shrugged, rose and walked to the Hallicrafter, picked up the disconnected plug and thrust it into the socket. I snapped the dial on. "Watch."

The panel flashed and darkened; confused static came crackling from the speaker. I took my hand away.

"Turn it up," said Andy uneasily.

"It's already up." My hand twiddled the dial.

"Try another station," the kid insisted. I pushed each button in succession; the static crackled and buzzed; the panel light flashed on and off in little cryptic flashes. I said "And reception was fine at noon; you were listening to the President's press conference." I took my hand away again. "Okay, you try it."

Andy frowned, but he came over and switched the button back on. The little panel light glowed steadily, and the mellow voice of Milton Cross filled the room:

"... orchestra in the Fifth, or Fate Symphony of Beethoven ..."

And then the majestic chords of the symphony, thundering through the cabin:

"Ta-da-da-*dumm*. ... ta-da-da-DOOM!"

My brother stared at me as racing woodwinds caught up with the brasses. There was nothing wrong with the radio. I stood listening to the sound of fate.

"Mike. What did you do to it?"

"I wish I knew." I reached out; touched the volume button briefly.

Beethoven died in a muttering static of insane drums.

I swore, and Andy sucked in his breath between his teeth, edging warily backward. He stared at the radio and then at me, and then reached out and touched the dial. Once more the smoothness of the

"Fate" symphony rolled out into the room and swallowed us. I shivered.

Andy said, shakily, "Maybe you'd better let it alone."

The kid turned in early, but I stayed in the main room, smoking, restless, wishing I could get a drink without driving eighty miles over bad mountain roads. Neither of us had thought to turn the radio off, and it was moaning out some interminable, throbbing jazz. I turned my notes over restlessly, not really seeing them.

Lightning that wasn't lightning. Scars on my body —curious festering marks that the psychiatrist had tried to tell me were psychosomatic. The cry of an eagle wheeling above me—*striking savagely at my eyes, set to kill*—and *I deserved that death.*

What had I remembered, just then, when I went for the eagle with a hunting knife?

I let my head sink in my hands, closing my eyes, trying to clear my mind of surface things and remember ... remember. ...

Fantasy? Was it fantasy that made me see a strange, cloaked form, and between the cloaked form and me, a woman? A golden woman. ...

Golden hair, tiger-tawny, fell like silk around her shoulders; her eyes were golden, wide open and fixed on me like the eyes of a great cat. She held something in her hands.

Vision, dream, fantasy—abruptly she was gone as Andy's voice came sleepily from the alcove:

"Going to read all night, Mike?"

"If I feel like it," I said tersely, and began walking up and down again.

"Michael! For the luvvagod *quit* that and let me get

some sleep," Andy exploded, and I sank into the armchair again. "Sorry, Andy."

Where had the intangible part of me been, those hours and days while I lay crushed under a fallen beam in the lab, then under morphine in the hospital? Where had those scars come from—and where had they gone?

More important—what had made a radio lab, of all places, explode like that? Electricity can set fires, and radio waves, too intense, will inflict burns. Men can be shocked into insensibility, or even killed, by electricity. But electricity just doesn't *explode*.

And what freak of lightning was I carrying in my body, that made me immune to ordinary current? I hadn't told Andy about the time I'd deliberately shorted the dynamo in the cellar and taken the whole current through my body. I was still alive. It would have been a hell of a way to commit suicide, but I hadn't.

I swore, slamming down the window. I was going to bed. Andy was right; either I was crazy, or else there was something wrong that ordinary doctors didn't know about. Sitting here stewing about it wouldn't help. If it didn't let up, I'd take the first train home and see another psychiatrist—and if that didn't help, well, maybe I'd see a good electrician! But right now, I was going to hit the sack.

My hand went out automatically and switched off the light.

"Damn!" I thought incredulously; I'd shorted the dynamo again. The radio stopped as if the whole orchestra had dropped dead; every light in the cabin winked swiftly out, but my hand on the switch crackled with a phosphorescent glow as the entire house current poured through my body. I tingled with weird shock, heard my own teeth chattering.

And something snapped open in my brain. I heard, suddenly, an excited voice, shouting.

"Rhys! *Rhys!* That is the man!"

CHAPTER TWO

"You are mad," said the man with the tired voice.

I was drifting. I was swaying, bodiless, over a vast abyss of caverned space; chasmed, immense, limitless. Vaguely, through that humming distance, I could hear two voices. This one was old, and very tired.

"You are mad. They will know. Narayan will know."

"Narayan is a fool," said the second voice. There was something hauntingly familiar about that voice. I had heard it before. *Where?*

"Narayan is the Dreamer," the tired voice said, "he is the Dreamer, and where the Dreamer walks they will know. But have it your way. I am old, and it does not matter. I give you this freely to spare you, and to spare Gamine what must come."

"Gamine—" the second voice stopped. After a long silence, "You are old and also a fool, Rhys. What is Gamine to me?"

Bodiless, blind, I drifted and swayed and swung in the sound of the voices. The humming, like a million high-tension wires, sang around me, and I felt myself cradled in the pull of something like a giant magnet, that held me suspended securely on nothingness, and drew me down into the field of some force below—

above—*elsewhere*. Far below me the voices faded, and as if their sound had removed some invisible and intangible support, I swung free—fell—plunged downward in sickening motion, head-over-heels into the abyss. ...

And yet, through all this, I was conscious of standing motionless, my hand on the light-switch in the cabin—and yet I was falling through nowhere space ....

My feet struck hard flooring with a kind of snap. I wrenched back to full consciousness with a jolt. Winds blew cold in my face: the cabin walls had been flung back to the high-lying stars. I was standing at a barred window at the very pinnacle of a tall tower, in the lap of a weird blueness that arched flickeringly in the night. I caught a glimpse of a startled face, a lean tired old face beneath a high, peaked hood, in the moment before my knees gave way and I fell, striking my head against the bars of the window.

I was lying somewhere in the dark. I had no awareness of myself as Mike Kenscott; instead my mind was filled with a nightmarish fear and urgency. There was something I had to do, a warning I had to give. ... and I was horribly afraid.

I stirred and around me the darkness thinned and grew paler; I could see, dimly, shapes and forms. I rose, with the fluid motion of movement in a dream, passed through a strangely arched door and into a dim-lighted corridor, burning with blue fluorescence. My own breath was loud in the silence, but I heard no footsteps. I knew I must be very still and keep to the edges of the corridors, and at the same time something angry and proud in me told me to walk fearless and unafraid.

The corridor was long, but I felt no fatigue. Twice I passed strange forms, feeling no curiosity about their strange cloaked and muffled shapes; I knew somehow that they could not see me. I paused before a bolted door, and the frightened part of myself stopped, feeling dreamish panic. Then I felt myself raise my hands, making curious gestures. The door slid noiselessly back and I passed through.

The room was dark and empty, with a great window opening on starred night. Here and there around the walls hung strange limp winged forms. Without hesitation I went to the wall and lifted down one of the things. ...

A cloak? A dead bird? I felt feathers, pinions, limp and lifeless; a curious fear sucked under my breastbone. Some tiny packed-away part of me screamed, *What am I doing?* But without hesitating, I drew the dark feathered thing over my head. ...

There was a strange, suspended, timeless moment when I floated, bodiless, a mere point of consciousness in space. Then, fumbling, I found my body again, moving the feet carefully to a low couch; supporting myself with my hands, I lowered myself and lay down. There was a strange pull to my body, an awful tugging as if the essential me was struggling to get out, to free myself from tangled heavy clothes. I knew somehow that I dared not yield yet to this struggle for freedom. Carefully, painfully, I lowered myself to the couch, straightened my body into a careful line, drew a deep breath ...

And suddenly I was out and away, rising up with a great flapping of wings, soaring on the rhythmic beat of pinions. My arms—my arms were great wings, and all around me was empty sky and cold fresh winds.

Flying! The oldest dream of mankind—but this was no dream! I could feel the cold sting of the wind, laden with sprinkles of dampness. Dark as it was, my eyes swept down from the dizzy height and saw below me a vast tract of wooded country. Colors were filtered out in the moonlight, but far, far below me I saw a tower rising and the great black yawning window from which I had come.

Nightmarish haste beat at me; I felt my bird-body stretch itself into an arrow-straight line, felt the pinions extend themselves into regular beating. I was flying Eastward, over the woodland, seeing below me little roads and pathways, isolated dwellings and farmland, feeling the wind in my face.

It seemed hours that I flew, but I felt no fatigue, and the time seemed strangely telescoped, so that it might have been minutes or days. I passed the woodland, flying over hills and valleys, until at last, far below me, a cluster of tents and dwellings showed like dark shadows in the fading moonlight.

I banked against the breeze, began to fly downward in slow spirals. The freshening breeze in my eyes, the strengthening light, told me that dawn was near; the bird-body seemed tireless, the heart beating as strongly as an insensate machine, but I—the intangible *me*—felt fear and exhaustion and dread. I knew that the dawn brought danger for me; but I was not sure why.

Down, and down. A red line of light against the horizon crept and strengthened, giving color to the green meadowland below. Now I could see the tents clearly, and the men who were moving around them, coming out into the dawn.

Too late! I cried out and heard my voice a high, eerie falcon-scream; I had been seen. Below me the forms of the men clustered, broke into groups, cried out and pointed upward.

"One of their accursed spies!"

I saw a big man, formless in the dawn and featureless, kneel down, something like a crossbow athwart his chest. Suddenly fear gave way to rage. He dared! Wheeling, darting with a speed that amazed me, that made the ground below me into a blur, I plunged downward. The men scattered, crying out, and I heard my soundless laughter explode into another eerie bird-cry. ...

An arrow sang shrilly by me; another. Swiftly, automatically, I eluded them, but fear and wonder were rising in me. What was I doing here? Why had I come? Why were they shooting at me when I had come to warn ... to warn. ...

To warn—whom?

I saw the crossbow bolt speeding toward me, desperately beat wings to one side—too late! I braced myself for the shock.

The arrow went into my breast. Strangely, I felt no pain, only a curious sense of pressure; a tingling snap and a painful shock. I felt my wings go limp, collapse, heard a great outcry from the men below, joy and triumph and exaltation. I was falling. ...

With no sense of elapsed time, I was lying on a narrow high bed, in a room filled with doors and bars. I could see the edge of a carved mirror set in a frame, and the top of a chest of some sort. It was not the room where I had found—or dreamed?—the limp feather-forms. It was lighted with bright sunlight, and on a bench at the edge of my field of vision, two figures were seated.

One was an old man, an old, old, gray man in a

high peaked hood, hunched wearily beneath the cowl of a robe like a Tibetan lama's. Briefly I had seen the face beneath the cowl, heard the old, tired voice, in the moment before plunging into that strange dream? —of flight.

The other was a slimmer, younger figure, swathed in silken, silvery-blue veiling, with a thin opacity where the face should have been, and a sort of pale shining of flesh through the silken sapphire of the veils. The figure was that of a slim boy or an immature girl; it sat erect, motionless, and for a long time I watched it, curious, between half-opened lids. But when at last I blinked, it rose, and passed through one of the multitudinous doors; almost at once, a soft sibilance of draperies announced its return.

I sat up, getting my feet to the floor or almost there; the bed on which I was lying was higher than a hospital bed. The blue-robed creature gave me a handled mug, like a baby's drinking-cup; I took it hesitantly between my fingers.

"Neither drug nor poison," said the blue-robe mockingly, and the voice was as noncommittal as the veiled body; a sexless voice, soft alto, a woman's or a boy's. "Drink, and be glad it is none of Karamy's brewing."

I tasted the liquid in the mug. It had an indeterminate greenish look, and a faint pungent taste I could not identify, though it reminded me variously of anise and garlic. It seemed to remove the last traces of shock. I handed it back empty and looked sharply at the old man in lama costume, who had not moved at all, or even raised his eyes to look at me.

"You're—Rhys?" I said. "Where in hell have I gotten to now?" At least, that's what I meant to say. Imagine my surprise when I heard myself asking in a language I'd never heard before, but understood perfectly, "To which of the nine hells of Zandru have I now been consigned?"

At the same time I became conscious of what I was wearing. I wouldn't have been surprised to see feathers—if I was still dreaming—but there weren't any. I was wearing what seemed to be an old-fashioned nightshirt, chopped off an inch or so below the loins, and deep crimson in color. "Red flannels, yet!" I thought with a gulp of dismay, and checked my impulse to get out of bed. I didn't know how I'd come here, or who had put me into the thing, but I wasn't going to stand around in a red nightshirt!

"You might have the decency to explain where I am," I said, "and how I got here."

The tiredness seemed part of Rhys' voice. "Adric," he said wearily, "try to remember. You are in your own Tower. And you have been under restraint again. I am sorry." His voice sounded futile. I felt prickling shivers run down my backbone. In spite of the weird surroundings, the phrase "Under restraint" had struck home. I was a lunatic and locked up somewhere!

The blue-robe cut in, in that smooth, sexless, faintly-sarcastic voice, "While Karamy holds the keys to his memory, Rhys, you will be explaining it to him a dozen times in a cycle. He will never be of any use to us again. This time, Karamy won. Adric, try to remember. You are at home, in Narabedla."

It sounded like Bedlam; and it looked like it. I shook my head. Nightshirt or no nightshirt, I'd face this on my feet.

I felt better standing up. I walked to Rhys; put my

clenched hands on his shoulders. "Explain this! Who am I supposed to be? Where am I? You called me Adric. I'm no more Adric than you are!"

"Adric, you are not amusing!" The blue-robe's voice was edged with anger. "Use what intelligence Karamy has left you! You have had enough *sharig* antidote to cure a *tharl!* Now, who are you?"

The words were all but meaningless. I stared, trapped, and let my hands fall away from the old man. "Adric," I said, bewildered. No. I was Mike Kenscott. Hang on to that. Michael Warren Kenscott. Cabin in the Sierras. Fishing holiday with my brother Andy. *Andy!* Two times two are four. The circumference equals pi times the diameter. Four rulls is the chemming—*stop that!* Mike Kenscott. Army serial number 13-48746. I cradled my bursting head in my hands.

"I'm crazy. Or you are. Or we're both sane and this monkey business is all real."

"It is real," Rhys said, compassion in his tired voice. "He has been very far on the Time Ellipse, Gamine; never have I searched so far. Adric, you must try to understand. This was Karamy's work. She sent you out on a time-line, very far, very far into the past. Into a time when the world was different. She hoped you would come back changed, or mad. Or perhaps she simply wanted to punish you."

"Punish me for what? Who is—"

The weary, hunched shoulders went up and then down.

"How can I say what is between you and Karamy? Must I concern myself with that, too?" His eyes were dim, withdrawn. "I have done what I can. Now I must return to my own tower—or die. I have long outstayed my leave. Gamine, will you explain?"

"I will." A hint of emotion flickered in the neutral voice of the blue-robe—Gamine? "Go, Ancient."

Rhys left the room, silently, without turning back, or a word of farewell. Gamine turned impatiently to me again. "We waste time this way. Fool, look at yourself."

I strode to a mirror that lined one of the doors. Above the crimson nightshirt I sought for my own familiar face and the sight rocked my reason. Out of the mirror a man's face looked anxiously but the face of a stranger.

I clutched at the frame of the mirror with one hand. The man in the mirror did the same, as if in panicky striving to climb out of there. The face that was not mine was eagle-thin, darkly moustached, with sharp green eyes; and the body belonging to the face was lean and long and strongly muscled and not quite human. I squeezed my eyes shut. This couldn't be!

I opened my eyes. The man in the red nightshirt I was wearing was still reflected in the mirror, and he looked scared as hell. He was.

I turned my back on the mirror, walking to one of the barred windows to look down on the familiar outline of the Sierra Madre, a hundred miles away. I couldn't be mistaken. I *knew* those mountains.

But between me and the mountains lay a thickly forested expanse of land, which was like no scenery I had ever seen in my life. *Or had I seen it in that dream of flying?*

Dream?

The bars, I saw now, were not bars, but ornamental grilles; they opened, at a touch, onto a high balcony floored with blue slate. I was standing near the pinnacle of a high tower; I dimly saw the curve of another, just out of my line of vision, hardly more than a shadow. The whole landscape below me was bathed in a curiously pinkish light; through a heavy, overcast sky I could just make out, dimly, the shadowy disc of a watery red sun. Then—no, I wasn't dreaming, I really did see it—beyond it, higher in the sky and pale through the clouds, a second sun, so blindingly blue-white brilliant that even through the thick cloud-cover I had to squeeze my eyes shut and look away.

It was proof enough for me. I turned desperately to Gamine behind me. "Where have I gotten to? Where —*when* am I? Two suns—but I know those mountains."

The veiled face turned up to mine, question in the tilt of the shrouded head. What I had thought a veil was not that; it was more like a shimmering screen wrapped around the features, so that Gamine was faceless; an invisible person with substance but no recognizable characteristics. Yes, it was like that; as if an invisible person were wearing the curious silken drapery. But the invisible flesh was solid enough; fingers like warm steel gripped my shoulder:

"You have been back—back to the days before the second sun? Adric, tell me, was there truly only one sun, before the Cataclysm?"

"Wait," I begged. "You mean I've traveled in time?"

The exaltation slowly faded from Gamine's voice.

"Never mind. It is improbable in any case that you would remember enough—no, Adric, not really traveling. You were sent out on the Time Ellipse; you must have contacted someone in that Other Time.

Perhaps the contact lasted so long that you feel yourself someone else."

"But I'm not Adric!" I raged. Suddenly the words I had heard, in that sudden opening of my mind, came back to me: *That is the man.* The voice I now knew for Rhys had called him Adric.

"Adric sent me here, somehow! Maybe this is his body, but—"

I saw the blurring around Gamine's invisible features twitch. "It's never been proven that two minds can be interchanged that way. Adric's body—Adric's brain. The brain convolutions, the memory centers, the habit patterns—all those are part of the physical brain. You'd still be Adric. The idea that you are someone else is only an illusion of the conscious mind. It will wear off. You stayed too long, Adric."

I shook my head, puzzled. I was Mike Kenscott. I hung on to that, desperately. "I still don't believe it. Where am I?"

Gamine moved impatiently. "Oh, very well. You are Adric of Narabedla, and—if you are yourself again—Lord of the Crimson Tower."

"And who are you?"

"You don't remember me?"

"I don't."

"I am Gamine. I am a spell-singer—and other things."

I jerked my elbow toward the window. "Those are my own mountains out there," I said roughly, "but I'm not Adric, whoever he is. My name is Mike Kenscott, and all your hanky-panky doesn't impress me. Take off that veil, and let me see your face."

"I wish you meant that," a mournfulness breathed

in Gamine's soft contralto. "If I dared believe—"

A sudden fury blazed up in me from nowhere; without volition I took one step forward, and heard my own voice, shouting.

"What is it to you what I mean? What right have you to pry for that old fool Rhys? Get back to your own place, Spell-singer, before you find that Karamy has not all the magic in Narabedla!"

I broke off, appalled. What was I saying? Worse, what did I mean by it? Gamine turned; the sexless voice was merely amused. "Adric spoke then. Whoever sits in the seat of your soul, Adric, you are the same and past redemption!" The iridescent draperies whispered on the flooring as Gamine moved toward the doorway. "Karamy is welcome to her slave!"

The door slammed.

Left alone, I flung myself down on the high bed, stubbornly concentrating on Mike Kenscott, shutting out the vague and blurring mystery that was Adric impinging on my consciousness. I had spoken Adric's words. At least, they were not my words. But I was not Adric! I would not be! I dared not go to the window, and look out at the terrifying two suns, not even to see again the familiar, reassuring outline of the mountains, lest seeing them I should begin to believe...

But persistently the Adric memories came, a guilty feeling of a shirked duty, a frightened face—a real face, not a blurred nothingness—beneath Gamine's blue veil. Memory of strange hunts and a big bird borne on the pommel of a high saddle. A bird hooded like a falcon, in crimson. ...

Consciousness of dress made me aware of the— nightshirt?—I still wore. Moving swiftly, without deliberate thought, I found myself going to a door and sliding it open. I pulled out some garments and quickly dressed in them. They went on easily, strange though they were—tights, high gaiters, a laced tunic and overblouse—when I did not stop to think about what I was doing. Every garment in the closet was the same color, a deep-toned crimson, although some were edged with dark fur and a few were embroidered with gold or silver threads. A phrase Gamine had used broke the surface of my mind, like a leaping fish; Lord of the Crimson Tower. Well, I looked it.

There were knives and swords in the closet; I took down one to look at it, and before I realized what I was about, I had belted it across my hip. I stared, decided to let it remain. It looked just about right with the rest of the costume. It felt right, too. I was stepping back to get a better look when another door folded noiselessly back and a man stood looking at me.

He was young, and he would have been handsome in an effeminate sort of way, had his face been less arrogant. Lean, somehow catlike, it was easy to determine that he was akin to Adric, and to me, even before habit and memory fitted a name to him, and an identity.

"Evarin," I said.

He came forward, moving so softly that for an uneasy moment I wondered if he had pads like a cat's on his feet. He wore deep green from head to foot, similar in cut and material to the garments that clothed me. His face had a flickering, as if he could, at a moment's notice, raise about himself a barrier of invisibility like that which surrounded Gamine. He didn't look as human as I—as Adric.

"I have seen Gamine," he said. "I'm told you are awake, and as sane as you ever were. And we of Narabedla are not so strong that we can afford to waste even a broken tool like yourself. So welcome home, brother!"

Wrath—Adric's wrath—boiled up in me; it was an unnerving experience to feel myself boiling with rage against a man I'd never consciously seen before. I felt myself step forward, felt my hand grip around the hilt of my sword. Evarin moved lithely backward.

"I am not Gamine," he warned, "nor to be served as Gamine was served. Be careful!" he made no move to touch the knife in his belt.

"Be careful yourself," I muttered, not knowing what else I could have said. Evarin drew back his thin lips into a smile. "Why? You have been sent out on the Time Ellipse until you are only a shadow of yourself. But I did not come here for a quarrel, and all this is beside the point. Karamy says you are to be freed, so the seals are off all the doors, and the Crimson Tower is no longer a prison to you. Come and go as you please—at Karamy's bidding." His lips formed a sneer. "If you call *that* freedom."

I said slowly, "You don't think I'm crazy?"

"Except where Karamy is concerned, you never were," Evarin said. "What is that to me? I have all I could desire. The Dreamer gives me good hunting, slaves enough to do my bidding, and as for the rest— I am the Toymaker. I need little else. But you—" his voice leaped with sudden contempt, "you who were so powerful—now you ride Time at Karamy's bidding, and your Dreamer walks waiting the coming of his power that he may destroy us all one day!"

I stared somberly at Evarin; the words meant little

to me, a jumble about Karamy again and Dreamers, and yet they seemed to wake an almost personal shame in me. Were emotions, then, only a habit of the mechanical synapses of the brain? Had they no connection with the person I was, Mike Kenscott? Or was I mad—feeling the emotions of a person called Adric, shame and regret and fear over things I'd never done, or dreamed of doing?

Evarin watched me, and his face lost some of its bitterness. He seemed little more than a boy. He said quietly; "The falcon flown cannot be recalled. I came only to tell you that you are free." He turned, shrugging his thin shoulders that seemed somehow misshapen, and walked to the high grilled window. "As I say, if you call that freedom."

I followed him to the window. The mists were clearing; the two suns shone with blinding brilliance, and I had to turn my eyes away from the sky. By looking far to the left, I could see a line of rainbow-tinted towers rising, tall and delicate, yet massive, capped with slender spires. The nearest seemed to be made of jeweled blue, some stone that gleamed in the light like lapis lazuli; one, clear emerald green; others were golden, flame-orange, violet. They formed a semicircle about a wooded park, and beyond them the familiar skyline of the mountains tugged other memories. The blinding sky held no hint of blue, but was colorless as sunlight on ice. Abruptly I turned my back on it all.

Evarin murmured, "Narabedla. Last of the Rainbow Cities. Adric, how long now?"

I was trying to make sense of the names he had spoken. "Karamy"— I said hesitatingly, but Evarin took it for a question.

"Karamy can wait. Better for you if she waited forever," he said with that soundless laughter. "Come along with me, or Gamine will be back. You don't want to see Gamine, do you?" He sounded anxious, and I shook my head. No. Emphatically, I did not want to see that insidious spook again.

He looked relieved. "Come along, then. If I know Gamine, you're pretty well muddled—amnesiac. I'll explain. After all," his voice mocked, "could I do less, for my only brother?"

He thrust open the door, gesturing for me to lead the way. Instinctively I drew back, telling myself it was only because I did not know which way to go. He laughed soundlessly and preceded me, and I followed, letting the door slide shut.

We went down stairs and more stairs, and I walked along at Evarin's side, wondering with some surface part of my thoughts why I was not more panicky. I was a stranger in an incredible world, wearing another man's clothes, called by his name, led around by his friends, or his enemies—how could I tell which? And yet I had the fantastic calmness with which men do incredible things in a dream. I was simply taking one step after another, surrendering myself to—Gamine had called them habits, memory patterns embedded in the convolutions of the brain. Patterns? I had Adric's body and presumably his brain. It seemed to know what to do. Only a superficial me, an outer ego, was a strange, muddled Mike Kenscott.

The subconscious Adric was guiding me. I let him ride. I felt it would be wise to be very much Adric around Evarin, though he seemed friendly enough.

We stepped into an elevator shaft which went

down, curved around corners with a speed that threw me against the wall, then, slowly, began to rise. I had long since lost all sense of direction. Abruptly the door of the shaft opened, and we began to walk along a long, dimly-lighted corridor.

The corridor of my dream?

From somewhere we heard singing; a voice somewhere in the range of a trained boy's voice or a woman's mature contralto. Gamine's voice. I could make no sense of the words, but Evarin halted, swearing.

I thought the faraway voice sang my name, but I could not tell. "What is it, Evarin?"

He gave a short exclamation, the sense of which was lost on me. "Come along. It is only the spellsinger singing old Rhys back to sleep. You waked him this time, did you not? I wonder Gamine permitted it. He is very near his last sleep, old Rhys. I think you will send him there soon."

Without giving me a chance to answer—and indeed I had no answer ready—Evarin pulled me into another shaft which began immediately to rise with us. Eventually we stepped out into a room at the top of another tower, a room lavishly, even garishly furnished. Evarin flung himself down on a divan, gesturing me to follow his example.

"Now tell me, where in Time has Karamy sent you now?"

"Karamy?" I asked tentatively.

Evarin's raucous laugh rang out again. "Can you really be as confused as you sound? Ai, what a joke it would be on Karamy, if it were so! The Witch of the Golden Tower destroys your memory—even your memories of *her!*" He flung back his head, shaking with that eerie laughter.

Then, suddenly quieting, he said with an odd air of confiding, "My one demand of the Dreamer is freedom from that witch's spells. We in the Rainbow City should at least leave one another free. Some day—some day I shall fashion a Toy for her, and she will discover that the Toymaker of Narabedla is to be reckoned with. I demand little of the Dreamers, Zandru knows, I do not care to pay their price. But Karamy does not care what price she pays, so—" a spreading movement of his hands, "she has power over everyone, except me. She had power to send you out on the Time Ellipse. I wonder who brought you back?"

It was beginning to make an eerie sort of sense. Somehow, Adric had incurred the wrath of Karamy, who was a "witch of the Golden Tower," whatever *that* was, and she had sent him out of his body. Someone, in trying to bring him back, had snared—*me*.

But I wasn't going to tell Evarin that. Something deep inside me knew that a confession of weakness or fear would be a catastrophe. I only shook my head.

"Anyhow, I'm back," I said. "Though I don't remember much."

"You remember me," Evarin said. "I wonder why she left you that? Karamy never trusted me."

And she was right not to trust him. The thought came out of that reservoir of knowledge that I could not tap at will, but nevertheless welled up in me. I said "Only your name. Nothing more."

Because Evarin, I knew, was never ten minutes the same. He would profess friendship at one minute, and mean it; ten minutes later, still in friendship and with no malice in him, he would flay the skin from my body and count it only an exquisite joke. He seemed to follow my thoughts, laughing.

"Still, you know my name, and that is something—*bare is brotherless back*, and that goes for me as much as for you, Adric! Tell me what you have forgotten."

Could I trust him with my terrible puzzlement? How much could I, as Adric—and I must *be* Adric to him, for that was my only safety, his wary respect for Adric and what Adric might do—how much could I, as Adric, get along without knowing? And how many questions could I dare to ask without betraying my own helplessness?

"I've been out of my body too long," I said at last. "I can't remember." One thing, at least, I had to know, "What are the Dreamers?"

That had been the wrong question. I knew it as soon as it escaped my lips. His eyes altered; he felt safer with me, now.

"Zandru, Adric, you have been far indeed," he said. "You must have been back before the Cataclysm."

I had, whatever the Cataclysm was. But I only nodded.

"Well, our forefathers, after the Cataclysm, built the Rainbow Cities, and made the Compact that killed the machines. In the Rainbow Cities we who could be trusted with power, lived and ruled as we had always lived and ruled; but the Compact made it certain that lesser men would never again be able to defy us. Oh, there were a few idealists who said that we were reducing them to barbarism. They didn't understand!" Evarin sounded passionately excited. "It was only that we kept them safe—safe from powers they only abused! They live simply, as common men are meant to live, and they cannot meddle with arts and powers beyond their understanding!"

He looked at me as if in challenge, but I said nothing, and Evarin got up and began to pace the floor restlessly.

"What are the Dreamers? No one knows; they do not know, themselves. They were men once. At least, they are born from men and women. Mendel knows what caused them. But one in every ten thousand men is born such a freak—a Dreamer."

"Mutations?" I said the word only to myself; Evarin did not hear. He went on:

"Some say that they were caused by the Cataclysm itself; others, that they are the souls of the dead machines. They are human and not human. They are telepaths. They have power; they can control everything: things, minds, people. They can throw illusions around men and things—they contested our rule."

He sat down again, brooding, quiet. "A dozen generations ago, here in Rainbow City, one of our people managed to bind the Dreamers. We could not kill them—they can protect themselves, I do not know how—for the weapon aimed at them must fall; the blow turned upon them recoils upon the striker. But he learned how to bind them, in sleep, make them harmless to us. That in itself might have been enough. But then we discovered that as they slept—and dreamed—they could be forced to give up their powers. To us. So that we controlled their powers, could wield their magic." There was a glimpse of horror behind his eyes as he said, "For a price. The price you know."

I kept silent. I did *not* know the price. I wanted Evarin to go on.

He shivered a little, shook his head, and the horror vanished.

"So each of us in Rainbow City has a Dreamer who gives up his powers—for the price appointed—so that his master can do as he wills. And after years and years, as the Dreamer grows old and feeble, his powers wane, and then they can be killed. As they grow older and weaker, it is even safe to let them wake but never too strongly, or too long."

He laughed, bitterly. A fury came from nowhere into his face.

"And you loosed a Dreamer!" he cried. "A Dreamer with all his powers hardly come upon him! He is harmless as yet, but he waked, and he walks! And one day the power will come upon him and he will destroy us all!"

Evarin's thin features were drawn with despair, not arrogant now, but filled with fear and pain. "A Dreamer," he sighed, "and you had been made one with him already! Can you see now why we do not trust you, brother?"

Without answering, I rose and went to the window. This tower room did not look down into the neat little park, but on a vast tract of wild country. Far away, curious trails of smoke spiraled up into the abnormally bright sunshine, but a thick, cottony fog lay over the bottomland. There was a shine of lakes, patches of forest, bare hills. Against the sky I saw a bird wheeling, silent, hovering against the wind.

"Down there," said Evarin in a low voice, following me to the window, "down there the Dreamer walks and waits to destroy us all. Down there—"

But I did not hear the rest, for my mind completed it.

Down there is my lost memory. Down there is my life.

Somewhere down there I had left my soul.

CHAPTER THREE

I TURNED from the window. "Rhys is a Dreamer," I said, with slow certainty. "What is Gamine?"

Evarin nodded, ignoring the question. "Rhys is a Dreamer, yes," he said. "He is old now, so old he is near to mortal. So he wakes, and he walks. But once he was one of us, the only Dreamer ever born within Rainbow City. He will not harm his kindred; he is of our blood." Evarin cleared his throat. "So that Gamine takes what knowledge can be had from his old, old mind. And does not pay."

"But Gamine?"

Evarin still hesitated. "Karamy hates Gamine," he said at last, "and so no one sees Gamine's face. I ask no questions and I would not advise you to ask, unless you ask Karamy." A smile flickered on his mobile mouth. "Ask Karamy," he said gleefully. "She will tell!"

Karamy. She had been mentioned many times now, this Witch of the Golden Tower. Perhaps her memory lay in the same deep well that had fitted name and identity to Evarin when he stood before me. But it seemed safe to ask, "Why does Karamy hate Gamine?"

"My brother, if you cannot answer that, who can? Gamine and I have little love for one another, but on one thing we agree that Karamy's procession of slaves is monstrous, and that you are a fool, and worse, to pay for her desires. Karamy is far too fond of power in her own hands to pay to put it into yours. She has won every struggle between you so far—or why were you sealed within your own tower?"

"But I'm free now," I said.

He surveyed me, curiously. "Yes. It's possible you might be stronger than I think. If so, we might join forces, you and I, if you think Karamy is too strong for our good. I can help you recover your memory." Evarin's prowling footsteps made no noise as he came to my side. "See, I have made you a Toy."

He put something small and hard into my hand, a thing wrapped in silvery silks. I raised my hand curiously, untwisting the wrappings. They were smooth and colorless with a bluish cast, like Gamine's veiling, like no other fabric I had seen before.

Evarin backed slowly away from me. For an instant all I could see was a sort of blurred invisibility, like Gamine's face through the veil; then a sort of mirror surface became visible. It did not seem to reflect anything; rather, it was a coldly shining surface, cloudy, glittering from within. I bent to examine the pattern of the shadows that moved on the surface. There was a curious pull from the mirror, a cold that crept sluggishly through my hand, a familiar, *soothing* cold. My eyes bent closer—

A faint movement distracted me; Evarin was watching me, avid, eager, intent. Recognition crashed suddenly in my mind. Evarin's deadly Toys! I dashed the thing to the floor, giving it a savage kick. The blurred invisibility wavered; I caught sight of a tiny jeweled mechanism before the thing sprang back to blurring gray ice again. Evarin had backed halfway across the room; I leaped at him and collared him.

"My memory's not that bad," I grated. "Damn you, I'll tie the thing to your throat!"

Evarin's mouth twisted; suddenly his whole face writhed into a blur and I felt his whole substance evaporate from between my hands; I backed away just in time as he materialized, whole and deadly, too close.

"I go guarded," he jerked out. "My Dreamer does not wake!"

He stooped for the fallen Toy; I kicked it out of his reach, bent to retrieve it. "I'll keep this," I said, and wadded the insulating silks around it, thrusting it into a pocket. Evarin glared at me, helplessly. Suddenly the rage in his face gave way to malicious laughter and he stood rubbing his bruised shoulder, laughing and laughing. "Well, it was a good try!"

"Yes," I said, not laughing, "but this will stay in my pocket, and you'll stay solid for a while now, anyway! Toymaker! Damned freak!" I stormed out of the room, slamming the door behind me.

Now that Adric was back in control, I had no trouble discovering where I wanted to go. Some blind instinct led me through the maze of elevators, corridors, staircases. I passed servants quarters, kitchens, rooms full of things which I dismissed with a bare glance of disinterested familiarity. I would have been hopelessly lost if I had stopped to think where I was going, but finally I found myself in the open, the semicircle of rainbow towers rising around me.

Overhead the suns, red and white, sent a curious double-shadowed light through the neatly-trimmed trees. A little day-moon, smaller than any moon I had ever seen, peered over the shoulder of the violet tower. The grass under my feet was just grass, but the brightly-tinted flowers in mathematically regular beds were strange to me; huge, fleshy, too bright. Paths, bordered by narrow ditches to keep the pedestrians off the flowers, wandered in and out of this strange lawn. I accepted all this without conscious thought, but some scrap of memory made me avoid the ditches most carefully. As I remembered, there was an extremely practical reason for them.

Faint, shrill music tugged siren-like at my ears, wordless, like Gamine's crooning. Staring, I realized that the flowers sang. The singing flowers of Karamy's garden—Adric remembered their lotus song. A song of welcome? Or of danger?

I was not alone in the garden. Men, kilted and belted in the same gaudy red and gold as the flowers, passed and repassed restlessly, unquiet as chained flames. For a moment the old vanity turned uppermost in my mind. For all her slaves, Karamy paid homage to the Lord of the Crimson Tower! Paid—would continue to pay!

The men passed me, silent. They wore swords, but their swords were blunt, like children's toys. They were a regiment of zombies, of corpses. Their very salutes as I passed were jerky, mechanical.

A high note sang suddenly in the flowers; I felt, not heard, the empty parading cease. In a weird ballet they ranged themselves into blind lines that filed away nowhere. They were toy-soldiers, all alike.

And between the backs of the toy-soldiers and the patterned flowers I saw a man running. Another me, from another world, thought briefly of the card-soldiers, flat on their faces in the Alice-in-Wonderland garden of the Queen. Wonderland. I heard myself say, with half-conscious amusement, "They all look so much alike until you turn them over."

The man running between the ditched flower-beds was no dummy from a pack of cards. He wore dark breeches and a dark shirt, and he moved quickly and lightly. I heard the high shrilling note again from the flowers—the flowers? Staring, I realized that the man held a whistle between his teeth, and it was this, blended into the flower-song, which gave the shrill note. He beckoned, still running, leaped over a ditch and came to rest near me.

"Adric!" he called softly, "Karamy walks here. Just listen to the flowers! I was afraid I'd have to get all the way into the Tower to find you and Narayan couldn't guard me that far!"

He raised his hand, the whistle in it, and blew a soft, liquid trill, which blended into the purring flower-tones. Then, drawing a deep breath, he said matter-of-factly, "Aldones! Am I glad to see you! Narayan said he *knew* you were free, but none of us quite believed it. He's outside the gates. He sent me to help. Come on."

The sight of the man touched another of those live-wires in my brain. *Narayan*. The name hit another, a dull chord of fear, of dread and danger.

But I had come straight from Evarin. I knew the man. I knew the response he expected, but that brief glance into the Toymaker's mirror?—had set up a chain of actions I could not control. I tried to put out my hand in friendly greeting, and felt instead, with horror, my fingers at my sword-belt. I tried, without success, to halt the sword that flew, without volition, from its sheath.

The man backed away, eyes full of terror. "Adric—

no—the Sign—" he held up one hand, deprecatingly, then shrieked with agony, bent double, clutching at the severed fingers. I heard my own voice, savage, inhuman, the thin laughter of Evarin snarling through it:

"Sign? *There's* a sign for you!"

The man flung himself out of range, but his face, convulsed with anguish, held more stunned bewilderment than anything else. "Adric—Narayan swore to us that you were—you were yourself again."

I forced my sword back into its sheath. It didn't seem to want to go; I had to struggle as if it were a live thing, writhing out like a serpent. I stared without comprehension at the wound I had not wanted to inflict, at the darting heads of the flowers behind the man. I could not kill this man who had the name of Narayan on his tongue.

The flowers twitched, stirred, threw long, ropy tendrils out toward the man's bleeding hand. A quick nausea tightened my throat.

"Run!" I said urgently. "Run, or I can't—" The flowers shrilled. The man threw back his head, eyes wide with panic, and screamed.

"Karamy! Aieee!" He staggered back wildly, teetering on the edge of the little ditch; I cried another warning, incoherent, too late. He trod on the flowers, stumbled across the little ditch. The writhing flowerheads shot up shoulder-high. They screamed, a wild paean of flower-music, and he fell among them, floundering, sprawling. I heard him scream once, harshly, hopelessly. I turned my eyes away. There was a wild thrashing, a flailing, a horrible yell that died and echoed against the walls of the enclosing towers. There was a sort of purring murmur from the flowers.

Then the flowers stilled and were quiet, waving innocently behind their ditches.

Karamy, gold and fire, walked along the winding path between the trees. And in the space of a second I forgot the man who lay in the bed of the terrible flowers.

She was all gold. From the glowing crown of her hair to the tips of her sandaled feet, she was a burnished shimmer; there was amber on her brows and a rod of amber twisted in her hand, and her smile was a dream. ...

A vision, a fantasy I had seen in my other world. ...

Great beauty has a stunning effect. It paralyzes other emotions. So I stared at the golden witch, at the shining amber rod that seemed to outline my face. But old habit made me turn my eyes away.

Karamy smiled, turning her cat's eyes to the lifeless sprawl in the flowers. "So? I thought I heard something. I wonder how he came so far?" Still watching me, she spun the shining rod; the flower-song rose again, a soft keening wail, and two of the zombie guards moved noiselessly through the garden. At the silent movement of the amber rod, they lifted the corpse and bore it away. The music died. Karamy's eyes were bent on the ground; following the direction of her glance, I saw something lying there. A whistle.

Karamy touched it with one sandaled toe. "Clever," she said scornfully, "but not quite clever enough."

Then, eagerly, she raised her face to mine and held out her delicate hands.

"Adric! Adric! As soon as you are free, they pursue you again! That is not what you want, is it?"

I didn't answer. One of Adric's memories scuttled

rabbit-fashion across my mind, giving a name to the man I had betrayed to the flowers.

Karamy slid in front of me so that I had to look at her. The lovely lazy voice murmured the name I was beginning to know.

"Adric, you are angry," the soft voice caressed me. "I knew it was cruel to let Evarin near you, but what else would have roused your anger enough to bring you back to yourself? Adric, we need you, Narabedla needs you. We felt betrayed when you left us, to shut yourself up alone with old Rhys and the stars! But now you have returned." Her hands gripped my shoulders and she clung to me. "Have you forgotten me, too? Or are you still my lover?"

It rang phony! Phony, was the way I put it to myself! Part of me felt like ripping her loose, calling her a lying, murdering she-devil, and getting that much, at least, on the record. But I was fast acquiring a double cunning. The animal cunning of Adric's old habit—and a desperate, trapped cunning of my own, born of fear—fear of this unfamiliar world with terrible dangers at every corner, and magic lurking in mirrors and flowers. And how could I tell what I, myself, would do next? There was blood on my hands already. And if Adric was a pawn between warring forces in this world, how could I know what to do? There was nothing to do except ride along on the surface, play my hunches, and see where they took me.

I said, "Who could forget you, Karamy?"

She was very soft and sweet and something more than lovely in my arms, and I held her crushingly close while I struggled with a memory that would not quite come.

Karamy dropped her arms. The mantle of lazy seductiveness dropped with them. "You are still angry because I sent you out on the Time Ellipse! You do not yet know it was for your own good! You have not yet learned your lesson!"

I retorted, "If I were a tame cat, would you have any use for me?" and pulled her back again. That talk meant danger for me; I could think of only one way to silence it. She seemed to like it, but even with her lips acquiescent under mine, I was wary. Was I fooling her, or was she just playing my own game, and playing it a little better?

And my mind was not completely on what I was doing. I was still aware of the fleshy, deadly, waving flowers. ...

"Now we can make plans," she said, a little later. "First, Gamine." She looked sharply at me, but I kept my face expressionless, and she went on, "Gamine is always with the old Dreamer; she lets him wake far too long. He is old; he is akin to us, but even so he will grow too strong. We must send Rhys away from Narabedla. Gamine may stay, or follow him to exile, but Rhys must go."

"Rhys must go," I conceded.

"He should be slain, but Gamine will never do it," said Karamy, with a shrug that disposed of Rhys, "and at least, while Gamine is bound to Rhys, Gamine seeks no bond with a stronger Dreamer. Evarin—" she snapped her jeweled fingers. "His Dreamer sleeps sound! Evarin fears even his own powers! As for his Toys, well, they can serve us too. My Dreamer grows strong but he serves me!" The beautiful face looked ruthless and savage.

"Your Dreamer walks free in the forest! Only you

can rebind him! You with my help, Adric of the Crimson Tower!" Her eyes smoldered. "Yes, and my Dreamer shall serve you, too, until then! I will pay to put power into your hands!"

The very phrase Evarin had used! Briefly, a shudder stung me. But Karamy's glowing face burned through the sting of fear.

"You have come back to us, Adric and we need you! Tonight, tonight I go to the Dreamer's Keep, and you go with me. And after that, you will go to the forest where the Dreamer walks and end this danger to Rainbow City forever! And then," her lambent eyes burned, a flame, a coal, "then there will be no challenge to our power, in all Narabedla, in all the world!"

Against my will, I felt the slow kindling of the flame she roused. Power, power unlimited, and a beautiful woman with sorcery at her fingertips. Adric's ambition was like a fire in me, and I was swept away on it.

Witch—golden witch! I knew now, how the Dreamers must be paid—the price for which they would give up their magical powers into the hands of the Lords of the Rainbow. The small part of me that was still Mike Kenscott shuddered away in fear and disgust; the rest of me accepted the memory with a shrug, and it was this Adric part of me that spoke.

"I'll go. I need power badly enough to take it even from your hands, Karamy. And afterward I'll go into the forest where the Dreamer walks, and bring him back to you."

But even as I swept Karamy into my arms and bent her head back roughly under my mouth, a warning prickle iced my spine, and my eyes narrowed over her golden head.

I said, insinuatingly, "And then, Karamy—" but only in my mind did I complete the sentence:

And then, Golden witch—I will find a way to deal with you, too!

CHAPTER FOUR

AFTERWARD, WHEN I had found my way back to the Crimson Tower, I searched for hours for something that might give a clue to Adric's mysterious past. I was puzzled about this Adric, this strange cotenant who came and went as he pleased in the chambers of my memory.

What was identity anyhow? Was it just an awareness of self? *I felt* like myself—like Mike Kenscott. I could remember living a whole life as Mike Kenscott, childhood, school, army, work, girls. And yet, and yet, with Evarin, with Karamy, with the strange man I had betrayed to the flowers, I had found myself acting, speaking, thinking in ways that Mike Kenscott could never have accepted.

I didn't want to think about that. If I stopped to think about it, I'd start to panic again. Grimly, I rummaged the rooms for clues. I found many strange things, but nothing of importance. Whoever had taken Adric's memory (Karamy? Why?) had made sure that nothing in his surroundings should clear up the puzzle in his mind.

I knew only one thing; Adric was feared, disliked, distrusted by all the Narabedlans, except, perhaps, Evarin in some moods. And all the Narabedlans except Gamine had something to gain by feigning friendship for Adric. I could not quite make out whether Karamy's attitude was love that pretended scorn to mold Adric to her will, or contempt that pretended love for the same reason. I didn't trust her, and I was just as glad that Adric didn't.

The name *Narayan* stuck burrlike in my mind. Friend or enemy?

The white sun had set, and the red sun was beginning to dip downward, when a servant knocked softly at the door, bringing food. He was not one of the zombies of Karamy's garden, but he spoke with respect verging on terror. Briefly, I considered questioning the man; then decided that I didn't dare. It would be foolhardy to let anyone in this rabbit-warren of enemies guess how weak, how confused and unsure I was. They thought that the Lord Adric was himself again, and if they were afraid enough of Adric, it might keep them off me for a while!

The man hesitated before backing out. "The Lady Cynara wishes to come to you, Lord Adric," he muttered at last. "May I bring her here?"

And who the devil was the Lady Cynara? Adric's wife? His concubine? Another of the Narabedlans, friend or foe, inhabitant of one of these Rainbow Towers? Whoever she was, I had enough trouble now. I said curtly "No," and the man mumbled something and went away.

I sat at the barred window of Adric's high tower, trying to force memory from the alien mind in which I was prisoner. And whether it was sheer effort of will, or the result of that fragmentary look in Evarin's mirror, or whether, as Gamine insisted, I was really Adric, and Mike Kenscott only an illusion of Karamy's magic, memory did begin to pulse back.

In the early days ...

In the early days, before the vagueness that came on my mind, Adric of the Crimson Tower had been a powerful lord of Rainbow City. The memories of that time were not memories which I, as Mike Kenscott, would have cared to own, but I, as Adric, found them vastly pleasing.

We were an ancient race, we lords of the Rainbow City. Our kin had wielded power over all this land, but we were a shrinking race, too, and a dying race. Fewer and fewer of the Children of the Rainbow were born to Narabedla's power. And of those, some were weaklings, unfit to share in the tremendous power of the captive Dreamers, and Adric, in his overpowering ambition, had struck against them, gathering all rule into his own hands. As kings in all lands have done from time out of mind, slowly, methodically, he eliminated all those who would contest his power. And now all Narabedla looked to the Lord of the Crimson Tower for rule; and in Rainbow City there dwelt only Evarin, who toyed with pleasure and mischief, and Gamine—had Adric ever known the truth about Gamine?—who loved only wisdom, and a scant handful of others who acknowledged Adric as unquestioned lord.

And Karamy! Karamy who had come to challenge my power—and remained to share it!

I had wanted power and I had had it, unlimited, from a Dreamer newly bound, who stirred but vaguely in his sleep. Past Narabedla, half the known portions of this world sent tribute to the Lord of the Crimson Tower.

Some memories were triumphant. Some seemed funny to Adric's cynical mind. Some were terrible beyond guessing, for Adric had not counted the cost of his triumphs, and even he shuddered at the price the Dreamers had exacted.

Then, to this willful and wild man, something had happened. I had no idea what. Fleeting images came through grayness—a blonde, boyish face lifted in incredulous terror, or joy: a fleeing form, veiled, that retreated down the corridors of my memory, averting its face as I followed.

Whatever had happened, it had come when Adric was surfeited, even if momentarily, with conquest, when he was sickened with blood and horror at the price of his power. For this magical power—forced through the mind of the Dreamers, the mutants, kept in enforced sleep or suspended animation—called for energy, kinetic energy, available from one source and from one source only, Adric had fed the Dreamer liberally with that source. For a time.

One day, as a whim, I had redeemed a young woman marked for that fate. Then the vagueness came and choked memory. I might think, I might burst my brain, but so far and no further could I remember. I could not force memory of that chain of events.

But after that, Adric's reign had collapsed like an arch with the keystone removed. His armies scattered; he had shut himself up or been imprisoned in the Crimson Tower, his memories had been stolen, and he had gone, or been sent, spinning along a time line, forward or perhaps back, whether in Time or Space I could not imagine, until somewhere in the abyss of the other worlds he had touched the man who knew himself as Mike Kenscott.

And then, perhaps, Adric had escaped. He had

reached out, drawn Mike Kenscott into his web and exchanged the two. It was a perfect escape, perhaps, for a life Adric had come to hate; a life filled with too many conflicts to be endured.

But I was Adric. ...

There was an explanation for that, too. The physical body could not make the transition. I had Adric's body, the convolutions of his brain, the synaptic links of habit. His memory banks. Only the ego, the superimposed pattern of conscious identity—the soul, if you will—was that of Mike Kenscott. In Adric's body and brain, the old patterns and habits ruled and, to all intents and purposes, I *was* Adric.

And back in my own time, I supposed, Adric was living in my body, living Mike Kenscott's life, going through the motions, with only the same queer lapses I was making here. And after a while, even these would fade. I was wholly trapped. Living Adric's life, would Adric grow stronger and stronger in me, until —he?—wholly unseated the other identity? And he, with my body, somewhere in the other world, would *he* become *me?*

Andy, I thought with a wild swift fear, *what will he do to Andy?*

Nothing. He could not harm Andy, not in my pattern, any more than I could hate Evarin. Or could he? I had drawn my sword, today, on a man who called me friend, given him to Karamy's terrible flowers.

I had to get back! God, I had to get back! But how? How had I come here?

Once before, for a little while, Adric and I had touched lives on—what had Gamine called it? The Time Ellipse. That day they thought the lab was struck by lightning. For eighteen hours, while I lay crushed under a laboratory beam, and later under drugs in the hospital, he and I had shared a fragment of life somehow. But the escape had not been complete. Something had driven him, or drawn him, back to his own world.

And he had tried again, or had been sent back. And this time he seemed to have succeeded. Was he in my hunting cabin in the mountains, cleaning fish for supper, curiously rummaging through my electrical equipment? Viciously I hoped he'd give himself some damned good shocks on it.

Something of Adric had stayed with me after our first contact. The strange lapses, the day I had flown at an eagle with my knife.

When the red sun glowed like a darkening ember across the Sierras, one of Karamy's toy-soldier guards came with a summons. Flat, mechanical, the words were a simple request for my presence, but they made me shudder. Somehow I had thought that these —zombies?—could not speak. I stared at the man. He was a tall sturdy looking fellow, with a round simple freckled face, bronzed with health; arms and chest were bulging with muscle. But the eyes were random, unfocused, the mouth was drooping-slack, and when I questioned him about where I was to go he stared and shifted his eyes and repeated in the same flat tone:

"The presence of the Lord Adric is requested."

He stood without moving, immobile except for the slow rise and fall of his breath, and finally it dawned on me that if this creature had no volition, he—or it— was simply waiting for my command. I wanted to tell it to go away, but I wasn't sure whether I could find my way without a guide.

I went automatically to the cupboard, drew out a crimson cloak lined thickly with fur, and shrugged it around my shoulders with a careless gesture; then—waved my hand at the silent sentry and he turned, his slow even tread ringing on the stairs. I followed him down through a labyrinth of stairs and elevator-shafts, finally emerging into a long corridor.

I strode down it, hearing my own steps echo; a second rhythm joined my steps, almost imperceptibly, and Gamine stole out of the darkness, still luminously veiled, a noiseless ghost behind me. Later I became conscious of Evarin's padding cat-steps trailing us. And others came from darkened recesses to stretch the silent parade; a girl in a slim-winged cloak the color of flame, a dwarfed man who walked in a huddle of purple cloak and dark fur.

The corridor began to angle upward, climbing toward a gleam of light at the end. Without realizing it, I had swung into an arrogant, loping stride; now I brushed away the slave-soldier who headed the column, and took the lead myself. Behind me the others fell into file as if I had bidden them; the flame-clothed girl in the winged cloak, Evarin in leaf-green, the dwarf bent in his jester's cap, shrouded Gamine. Without warning we came into a vast courtyard, an enclosed plaza of imposing grandeur.

The red sun glowed above us like a gas fire. There were tall pillars on three sides of the court, and at the far end a vaulted archway, leading into a tree-lined drive that stretched away, shadowy, into the forest. Between two pillars Karamy waited, slim, shimmering, golden; a hungry impatience sparked her cat's eyes.

"You're late!"

"I'm ready now," I said. For what, I wasn't sure.

Karamy waved an impatient signal to the Narabedlans who were coming up. "Adric is with us again! Your allegiance to Adric, Children of the Rainbow!"

I stood at her side, mute, waiting, the guard of silent men behind us.

"Lord Idris!" Karamy summoned. The dwarf came to bow jerkily before me. "Welcome home, Lord!"

Evarin's face was sly and malicious, but his voice was a purr of silk. "It is pleasure to follow you again, my brother."

The girl in flame-color said nothing, but her dipping curtsy was like the waver of a moth toward a flame. "Adric—" she murmured. She was a shy thing; the wings of her cloak lifted and fluttered as if they would fly of themselves, and her dark hair waved softly as if it too were winged. I touched her fingers lightly, but under the smolder of Karamy's eyes let her go.

"You ride with us, Cynara?" Karamy sounded displeased. The girl in the winged cloak raised her face, but she did not speak. Gamine's voice, a soft singing croon, hummed for a moment, almost wordless, in the twilight. Then, gliding forward, Gamine murmured, "It is my will, Karamy. Do you dispute my right?"

For a moment the tension was like visible force, like a shimmer in the air; then Karamy made a careless gesture.

"What do I care for you or your spells, Gamine? Come or go at your own will, bring whoever you like. There is no talk of rights at this moment."

I had wondered, seeing the Narabedlans assembled, if old Rhys would join us as well, but apparently he was not expected. From somewhere the silent men brought horses. Horses here in this nightmare world? They looked like any other horses anywhere. I had never been on a horse in my life. I found myself vaulting, with a nice co-ordination of movement, into the high, peculiarly horned saddle.

The courtyard, in spite of the stamping horses, the bustle of departure, somehow held the silence of the grave. Karamy kept me close to her; when we were all mounted, she flung the amber rod upward. The last rays of the sun caught its prism, and threw a beam of pure light down the darkened alleyway of trees. At the sight of that gleam, a curious emotion stole through me, at once familiar and strange. I flung up my arm over my head.

"Ride!" I cried. "Ride to the Dreamer's Keep!"

The alleyway under the arch of trees led for miles under the thick boughs. Behind us drummed the hooves of Karamy's guard; through the noise I could still hear the sweet floating sound of Gamine's singing, rising and falling with the rise and fall of the rolling road. The wind whipped Karamy's golden hair into a pale halo around her head.

I glanced back over my shoulder to where the rainbow towers stood, just black silhouettes now against the greater darkness of the mountains behind them. Overhead in the pink sky the crescent of the tiny moon was brightening; lower, near the horizon, I saw a wider disc, almost at full, just coming clear of the trees. Cold air was stinging my cheeks and nipping my bones with frost. I felt the sparks struck from the hooves beating on the frozen ground.

Frost! Yet in Karamy's garden, the flowers had

glowed in tropical glory!

And for a moment it was Mike Kenscott, entirely Mike Kenscott, sick, bewildered and panicky, who glanced about him with horror, feeling the swirling cold and a colder chill from the golden sorceress at my side. It was Mike Kenscott's will that jerked the reins of the big gelding, to end this farce now.

"What is it?" Karamy cried, above the hoofbeats.

And I heard my own voice, raised above the galloping rhythm, cry back, "Nothing," and call out a command to the horse.

Good God! I was Mike Kenscott, but prisoner in a body that would not obey me, a mind that persisted in thoughts and habits I could not share, a soul that would carry me to destruction! I was Mike Kenscott and I was trapped on a nightmare ride through hell!

CHAPTER FIVE

I HAD BEEN SCARED before. Now I was panicked, wild with a nerve-destroying fright. I'm no coward. I set up a radar transmitter on Okinawa within ninety feet of a nest of Japs. That was something real. I could face it. But under two suns and a pair of strange moons, surrounded by weird people that I knew were not human as I understood it—all right I was a coward. I steadied myself in the saddle, trying with every scrap of my will to calm myself. If this was a nightmare well, I'd had some beauties.

But it wasn't, I knew that. The frost hurting my face, the sound of shod steel on stone, the vivid colors all around me—dreams are not in color. All these things told me that I was awake, wide awake. And through all this I was riding hell-for-leather, knees gripped on the saddle, guiding the horse with the grip of my thighs, and I'd never been on a horse in my life. Riding, riding—

We had ridden several miles, and stopped twice to breathe the horses, but we were still beneath the great archway of trees. The sky's pink sunset had faded; the land was flooded with blue, fluorescent moonlight. I looked up through the black foliage; I suppose I had some confused idea that I might find out, when I was by the stars. But the view to the north was hidden by mountains, and except for the Big Dipper, I don't know one constellation from another.

I had dropped back from Karamy's side until I rode between Gamine and the girl in flame-color. The spell-singer saluted me with a vague nod, but the girl in the winged cloak threw back her hood, and I saw dark eyes, watching me from a pure, sweet young face. Before the luminous innocence of those eyes, I wanted to cry out that I was not Adric, warlock of Narabedla, I was just a poor guy called Mike, I was just—me!

But it was Gamine who spoke; the musical voice was not raised, but carried easily to my ears. "You seem to be wholly yourself again."

I didn't know what to say. I shook my head.

Strangely, there seemed to be sympathy in the neutral voice. "If our memory halts, at least you will remember—perhaps too much—at the Dreamer's Keep."

"Gamine," I asked, "who is *Narayan?*"

I saw the blue robes quiver a little, and a curious flickering glint crossed the face of the girl in the winged cloak. But Gamine's voice was perfectly even.

"I have never seen anyone of that name. Perhaps Cynara could answer you, if you asked her."

I glanced at the girl—Cynara? But I did not put the question, for the name *Cynara* had suddenly touched another of those live-wires in my brain—or Adric's Cynara. Narayan. Narayan and Cynara. *If I could only remember!*

What would Cynara have said, if I had let the servant bring her to me, in the Crimson Tower? Was it too late to find out?

I looked up at the girl again, and something in me

said *No!* Damn it, I didn't want any more of Adric's memories!

Cynara had drawn her dark pony level with mine. She rode side-saddle, easily, straight and slender, as if she had been born to it; beneath the flame-colored cloak she was small and slim, and endearingly human, the only normal, human thing I had seen in this world! I felt like bursting out, telling her—

"Don't be frightened," Cynara said, and her voice was low and sweet, muted so that I could barely make out the words, and her lips hardly moved. "You won't have to go. It's all arranged."

"What—" I burst out, but she shook her head quickly, with a warning glance at Evarin, who was swiftly overtaking us.

Karamy turned in her saddle; beckoned to me, imperiously. For a moment I rebelled; then I touched my heels to the horse's flank and rode forward to rejoin Karamy.

For several minutes the road had been climbing, and now we topped the summit of a little rise and abruptly the trees came to a halt. We drew our horses to a walk.

We stood atop the lip of a broad bowl of land, perhaps thirty miles across, filled to the brim with thick dark forest. Far out, at the bottom of this valley, lay a cleared space, and in that space rose a great tower. Not a slender, fairylike spire, not one of the towers of Rainbow City. This was a massive donjon, thrusting heavy shoulders upward into the moonflooded sky, ancient, terrible.

The Keep of the Dreamers!

Something in me murmured "This is the forest where the Dreamer walks" or had the murmured words come from Karamy, at my side? She rode eagerly, her face taut, her slender hands clenched on the reins. Part of me knew the reason for her eagerness, and part of me wondered at it. For all this time I was Mike Kenscott, but a helpless Mike Kenscott, who watched himself without knowing what he would say or do next! Like those puzzling nightmares where a man is both actor and audience to some mummery being played, I watched myself say and do things as if I were twins. In effect, I suppose I *was*—

Karamy turned in her saddle to face me.

"You don't trust me!" she said vehemently. "I can feel it! What is it?"

"Have I reason to trust you?" I was not sure whether I spoke or Adric, cautious, watching myself.

I had expected her to flare into anger again; instead, a bewitching cat-smile spread over her features, and her gold eyes seemed to gleam in the light. She murmured, "Perhaps not," and her laughter was like a golden bell.

Then her face grew intent and eager.

"Adric, if you would stop to think, you would realize that I need you, that Narabedla needs your strength. Listen, Adric, everything has changed. The people are rebellious, even defiant. *I* can't lead armies against them! I ask you, have we ever had to ride with guards before, here in our own forest?"

I heard Evarin's harsh laugh behind me. "So, you would strip Adric of all his powers, then complain because you have no strong hand?"

"And little enough punishment," said the harsh voice of the dwarf Idris, drawing his horse level with ours. He glowered at me. "I hate you for a traitor, Adric, you, who freed a Dreamer and loosed all this upon us! I said you should die!"

"But you can see it was not needful that he should die," Karamy said, and looked at me as if seeking my support. "Surely you can see now, Adric, that what I did was only to bring you back to your senses—to save what I could."

"She's right," Evarin said. "We can settle our private quarrels later, Adric; just now we have a rebellion on our hands, and a Dreamer at large. If Rainbow City is to survive at all, we've got to forget the past. What Adric may have done in a moment of madness, he can un-do now. If you can't make peace, at least make a truce!"

"Adric," Karamy murmured. "Take me where the Dreamer walks."

I knew, with sudden surety, that because of some bond between the freed Dreamer and myself, I could do this. But something cautioned me to say only, "That bond is broken, Karamy. Did you not break it yourself? I have not forgotten that much," and for my reward I saw unsureness leap in her cat's eyes. So that shot had told; Karamy *had* tried to break the bond, and had succeeded, or thought she had. Now, when she thought Adric was enough her dupe to use that bond only for her private purposes, and not against her, she was guessing.

But this woman was past mistress of subtlety. She murmured, "The bond can be reforged, that I swear."

Ah, but I knew how far to trust even Karamy's oaths! "Forge it, then," I said bluntly, "but don't count on me to un-do what you did."

We had dipped down into the bowl of forest, and were riding through thick woods, along a road that struggled windingly, with many curves and sharp corners. Adric knew this country; his knowledge made Mike Kenscott shiver. He had hunted here, and for no four-legged game. As if Karamy read my thoughts, I heard her low laughter.

"So. My wrist aches for the feel of a falcon! We'll hunt here again, you and I!" The words gave me a quivering excitement, an insidious thrill.

Behind me I heard Gamine's chanting take on a new note. The words were still indistinguishable, but the very tone held warning. A pulse began to twitch jerkily in my neck.

Without warning, the road twisted and redoubled in an S-curve. Karamy and I spurred our horses and rounded the first bend in one racing burst of speed, swung round the second, and were fairly in the trap before we knew it.

It was the agonized whinny of my horse, and the jolt of my body automatically righting itself from the plunging of the animal beneath me, that made me realize we had ridden straight on a chevaux-de-frise. I yelled, cursing, shouting to Karamy to get back, get back, but her own momentum carried her on; I saw her light body fly out of the saddle and disappear. The others, rounding the curve, were fairly on the barrier already, and the place was a scramble, with riderless horses milling in a melee of curses and the screaming of women and the thrashing of feet. I was out of my saddle in a moment, thrusting Gamine's mount back from the stabbing points fixed invisibly against the dark barrier in the road, shouting to Evarin and Idris. Evarin leaped to my side, and I tore madly at the barricade. Idris bore down on me, mounted. "Go round," he shouted. I plunged through the underbrush at the side of the road, with hasty feet twice snaked by long creepers. Past the barrier, the road lay open and deserted and Karamy lay there in a shimmer of crumpled silk, motionless.

"Gamine, Evarin," I shouted, "no one's here! Karamy is hurt."

The head and shoulders of Idris' horse thrust through the thick brushwood at the edges of the path. "Is she dead?"

I bent, thrusting my hand against her breast. "Only stunned. Her heart's beating. Get down," I ordered, and Idris scrambled, monkey-fashion, from the saddle. I lifted the woman in my arms, but she did not move or open her eyes. Idris touched my arm.

"Put her across my saddle."

She was a limp dead weight in my arms, and as I laid her on the saddle she stirred and moaned. Suddenly, behind me, Idris cried out.

"What?" I asked sharply.

"I heard—"

I never knew what Idris heard. His head vanished as if snatched away by a giant's hand; a rough grip collared me, choking fingers clawed at my throat, a thousand rockets went off in my head, and I lay sprawling in the brushwood, eating dust, with an elephant sitting on my chest and threatening hands gouging at my throat. My last coherent thought, before the breath went out of me, was—

"I'm waking up!"

CHAPTER SIX

BUT I WASN'T. When I came to—it can only have been a few seconds that I was unconscious—it was to hear Evarin snarling curses, and Idris barking incoherently with rage. I heard Karamy shriek my name, and tried to answer, but the steely fingers were at my throat, and with that weight on top of me I hadn't a chance. The fall, or something, had knocked Adric clean out of me, I was fuzzy-brained, but I was *me*; I was an innocent bystander again.

I could just see Evarin and Idris in the road, casting wary glances into the thick brushwood. Above me, I could barely make out the face of the man who was holding me pinned to the earth with his body. He had the general build of a hippopotamus, and a face to match. I squirmed, but the threatening face came closer, and I subsided. The man could have broken me in two like a matchstick.

Around me in the thicket were dozens of crouching forms, fantastic snipers with weapons at their shoulders, weapons that could have been crossbows or disintegrators—or both. "Enter Buck Rogers," I thought wearily. I was beginning to feel faint again, and old welter-weight on my stomach didn't help any.

Just as I thought I'd burst, he moved, stubby fingers knotting a gag in my gasping mouth; then the intolerable weight on my chest was gone, and I sucked in air with relief. The fat man eased himself cautiously away, but I felt a steel point caress my ribs. The threat didn't need words.

I could see the Narabedlans gathered in a tight little knot in the road. The snipers around me were still holding their weapons drawn, but the fat man commanded in a whisper "Don't fire. They're sure to have guards riding behind them."

The voices died away to a rasping mutter, and I lay motionless, trying to dig up some of Adric's memories that would help. But the only thing I got was a memory of my own football days, and a flying tackle from a Penn State halfback that had knocked me ten feet. Adric was gone, clean gone.

The Narabedlans were talking in low tones, Gamine the rallying-point around which they clustered. I wondered why that surprised me; then the surprise, too, faded. Evarin had his sword out, but even he did not step toward the mantling thicket. Cynara was holding Idris by the arm, and I heard her crying out, wildly, "No, no! If you make a move, they'll kill him!"

Between two breaths, the road was alive with mounted men. I never knew who they were; I was quickly jerked to my feet and dragged away. Behind me I heard shouting, and steel clashing, and saw flashes of colored flame; spots of black danced before my eyes as I stumbled along between two of my captors. I felt my sword dragged out of the scabbard. *Oh well*, I thought wryly, *I don't know how to use it, anyhow, now that Adric's run out on the party!*

Under the impetus of a knife in my ribs I found myself clambering into a saddle, awkwardly, hands tied, felt the horse running beneath me. There wasn't much chance of getting away, and anyhow, the fire couldn't be much worse than the frying pan!

Behind us the sounds and scufflings died away. The horse I was riding raced sure-footed in the darkness. I hung on with my two hands; only Adric's habitual muscle reflexes kept me from tumbling ignominiously to the ground. I don't think I had any more coherent thoughts until the jolting rhythm broke and we came out of the forest into full moonlight and the glare of open fires.

I raised my head, still clinging to the saddlehorn with one hand, and looked round. We were in a grove, tree-ringed like a Druid temple, lighted with watch-fires and torches stuck up on long poles. Tents sprouted in the clearing, giving the place an untidy, gypsy appearance. At the back was a white frame house with a flat roof and wide doors.

I swallowed hard, swaying in the saddle, *It was the place of my dream, where I had flown as a strange bird, where an arrow had struck me.* I felt a strange darting pain in my chest, and grabbed at the horn of the saddle.

Men and women were coming out of the tents everywhere. The talk was a Pentecost of tongues, but I heard the name "Adric!" run in a blaze around the circle, and over and over again, another name, repeated:

"Narayan! Narayan!"

A slim young man, blonde, dressed in rough brown, came out of one of the larger tents and walked deliberately to me. The crowd drew back, widening to let him approach; before he came within twenty yards he signaled to one of the men, who immediately unknotted the gag from my mouth and untied my hands, helping me slide down from the saddle. I stood clinging to the stirrup, exhausted.

"Any trouble, Raif?" the young man asked.

My gigantic captor shook his head. "Seems we caught 'em without any magic! They were bound for the Keep, but we've kept 'em away a good while now. The Witch had a few dozen of her guards, though."

The blonde young man shook his head soberly. "At least you got safely away? You didn't try to fight."

"Orders are orders," said the big man glumly. "You said, get Adric and get away again. Well, here he is and here we are, and those—" he swore, shockingly, and the blonde young man laughed.

"You'll have your chance for fighting, soon enough!"

He came forward until he could almost have touched me, and studied my face dispassionately. At last he raised his head, turning to the fat man, Raif.

"This isn't Adric," he said, "I don't know this man at all."

I should have been relieved. I don't know why I wasn't. Here was somebody, at last, who could tell the difference. Instead, my first reaction was bewilderment and angry annoyance. How could he tell that? I was as furiously embarrassed as if I'd been caught wearing stolen clothing. My beefy captor was as angry as I was.

"What do you mean, this isn't Adric?" he demanded. "Are you wearing your eyes inside your pockets? We took him right out of their accursed cavalcade! If it isn't Adric, who is it?"

"I wish I knew," Narayan said under his breath. His eyes were still fixed on my face, with a stillness that was disconcerting. He was tall and straightly built, with pale blonde hair, square-cut around his shoulders like a troubadour in a Provençal ballad, and gray eyes that looked grave, but friendly. I liked his looks, but he had a trace of the uncanny stillness I'd noticed in old Rhys. For a moment I had half decided to tell my story to this man with the grave eyes. He would surely believe it.

But as he looked at me, doubt came into his face, and then he sighed and looked at the men around him before turning back to me.

"Adric?" he said, "do you still remember me? Or did Karamy take that, too?"

I sighed. I didn't dare tell the truth, and I felt too chilled and exhausted and disoriented to lie convincingly. Yet lie I must, and do it well, without even knowing why this man—Narayan?—had twice risked an attack on the powers of Rainbow City to get Adric away.

Well, I had an excuse in Adric's supposed loss of memory. Anything I didn't remember, any mistakes I made—"You are Narayan?" I asked.

The fat man, still holding me by the elbow, scowled at Narayan. "Don't let him get by with that," he growled. "Look you, did Brennan come back this afternoon? He knows his way around Rainbow City, he went guarded! Ask Adric what happened to Brennan and make him tell you!"

The clamoring broke out around us again, but Narayan never took his eyes from my face as he answered gently, "There is always danger, Raif. Blame no man unjustly. And even Adric is not to blame, if Karamy has him under her spells."

"Traitor!" Raif snarled at me, and spat. I had an

eerie memory of Idris—same words, same gestures. Around us the crowding men muttered to one another, casting uneasy glances at me, and I felt my body tensing, my fists clench with the first traces of the now-familiar, murderous rage of Adric. *Oh, God, no! Not again!* I thought of Brennan, his face raised trustfully to me in friendship, felt again the whiplash stroke of my sword, heard his dying yell. ...

Shaking, I clutched at the saddle-horn, trying desperately to hold on to myself. *Of all the people I might have been in this madhouse world, this Adric takes the prize,* I found myself thinking with a weird detachment, *neither side trusts him as far as they can kick him and I don't blame them.*

I let go of the saddle-horn and stepped dizzily forward. "You might try asking me," I said, with a weary anger.

"Then, if you're not Adric, who the hell are you?" fat Raif snapped, "and what did you do with Brennan?"

I shook my head, exhaustion sliding over me. I don't know what I would have said, but Narayan stepped toward me, saying quickly, "Not here, Raif." He seized my arm in a firm grip. "Stand back, you people there. Come along."

The men murmured to themselves, but they cleared a path for us, stepping back warily as Narayan led me toward the frame house at the edge of the grove; Raif and one other man trailed after us, and the men began to disperse into their tents and around their fires. A few, still grumbling, clustered hive-fashion round the door as we went up the steps.

Inside, in a great timbered room, a fire was burning; flames leaped up from a great crimson bed of logs, creating warmth and light in the shadows. I went toward the fire gratefully; I was stiff with riding, and chilled and empty and stupefied with the cold.

From a wooden settle near the fireplace, a slim figure rose, the figure of a slight dark girl in a cloak that caught the firelight like escaped flames.

"Cynara!"

"Adric," she said half-aloud, holding out both hands to me. I took them, partly because she seemed to expect it, partly because the girl seemed the only real thing in this whole incredible nightmare. *Something real, something to hold on to—*

Then she flung her arms around my neck and held herself close to me, not passionately, not sensuously, but, in a curious way, as if she were *protecting* me.

So she had known about this. But what was she doing here?

Narayan took the girl by the shoulder and gently pulled her away from me; she shrank a little before the annoyance in his eyes.

"Cynara," he said, "what are you doing here?"

"I—I slipped away from them in the dark. I suppose Gamine knows, but they'll never find me here."

He looked down at her, shaking his head. At last he said, "Little sister, you must go back to Narabedla. I would not make you go if there was any other way, but there is not. We have all risked too much to keep you there." He beckoned to the third man who had come inside with us. "Kerrel, take Cynara back to the roadway, but don't get caught yourself. Cynara, you can tell them that you were lost in the woods, or that you were caught and escaped."

"I won't go back," she said, with her mouth trembling. "Now that Adric's here again, what's the use of it? Surely there can be an end to it, now."

She clung to my hand, but I only shook my head, helplessly. I didn't understand, but her fear communicated itself to me. I put my arm round her, feeling her tremble. Narayan looked from Cynara's face to mine, and finally sighed.

"Maybe you're right. Now's the time when we have to risk everything, win all, or lose all." He turned to the men. "I'll talk to Adric. Alone."

Raif's thick lips set, stubbornly. He looked as if he'd be a very nasty customer in a fight.

"If he's Adric, and if he's under Karamy's devilments, then—"

"I have faced Adric, and Karamy too," said Narayan with a friendly grin. "Get out, Raif, you're not my bodyguard, nor yet my nurse."

The fat man accepted dismissal, reluctantly, and Narayan came to my side. Cynara let go my hand and withdrew to the settle near the fire. I was sorry to lose her support.

She, at least, trusted Adric. . . .

There was real friendliness in Narayan's smile. "Well," he said, "now we will talk, you and I. You cannot kill me, any more than I could kill you, so we may as well be truthful with one another. Why did you leave us again, Adric? And what has Karamy done to you this time?"

The room reeled around me. I put out a hand to steady myself; when the dizziness cleared, Narayan's arm was around my shoulders, and he was holding me up with a strength surprising in his slight frame. He eased me into a seat. "You've been pretty roughly handled," he said. "The men, well, they had orders.

But perhaps they carried them out with too much zeal. And if I know Karamy's ways, you've been heavily drugged for a long, long time." His eyes studied me, intently. "You don't look very glad to be here, but at least you didn't come in fighting. Maybe we can talk. Better come and have a drink. And when did you eat last?"

I rubbed my forehead. "I can't remember," I told him honestly. Adric's servants had brought food, but I hadn't touched it.

"I thought so. You look half starved," Narayan said. "That's what *sharig* does to you, as I have reason to know." He went into the next room, assuming that I would follow and that I knew my way around.

After the insanely furnished rooms in Rainbow City, I was a little surprised when the next room turned out to be a fairly ordinary and functional kitchen, equipped with items not too unlike those in my own world. *Well, after all, how many ways are there to design a stove? Or a table?*

Out of a relatively unsurprising icebox, (although it had an oval door) he assembled various cold foods, and poured liquid into an oddly-shaped handled cup, motioned me into a chair and set the things on the table. "Here, eat this," he said. "I know those damned drugs of theirs; you'll make more sense after you've eaten, and we've plenty of time to talk, all night if we choose." He saw me glance at the mug, laughed sketchily and poured himself a drink from the same bottle; he sat down opposite me, sipping it slowly. "Go ahead. Even if I felt like poisoning you, I wouldn't until I knew what Karamy was up to," he chuckled.

I laughed, too. Poison? When any of them could have shoved a knife into me, at any time during the last three hours? I started eating. I hadn't felt hungry, but with the first bite, I realized that I was famished. I had last tasted food some forty-eight hours ago (and that had been in another world); Adric, judging from the hunger I felt, had evidently fasted longer than that. I ate everything on the plate; Narayan sipped his drink and watched me, and when I finally pushed the empty plate aside, he put back his mug and said, "Now, what's happened? You're Adric—and you're *not*."

I felt better and stronger than I'd felt since Adric, with help from Rhys (but why? *Why?*) had catapulted me into this world. Narayan seemed friendly, but so had Evarin. Now I must talk fast and convincingly, before those searching gray eyes.

"I'm not sure," I said at last. "I don't remember much, just coming to myself, this morning, in the Crimson Tower. I think it was this morning. I was freed. Karamy wanted to take me to the Dreamer's Keep, and then your men came along. I didn't know whether I was being captured or rescued. I still don't."

I stared with purposeful blankness at Narayan, and he stared back; I could feel his debate with himself, what to do or say. Obviously an Adric sane and glib and possibly untruthful was a different thing than a man too bewildered and drugged and shaken to tell anything but the truth.

Finally Narayan said, "I'm not sure what I ought to do or say, Adric. There was a time when I could read your thoughts. Not now. The bond between us isn't as strong as it was. You know that."

I nodded. Adric's thoughts seemed to be surging back, insidiously, as if Narayan held the key to unlock them. *Fool, not to question me when he had me in his power! Soft fool!*

I clung with both hands to my awareness of Mike Kenscott. What crazy drama was going to be unfolded in the battlefield of my mind now?

"What did Karamy do?" Narayan asked.

My voice was as quiet as his own. "Karamy sent me out on the Time Ellipse." This much I knew from Rhys and Gamine. "She hoped I'd come back changed, or mad, or maybe not at all. I think—I think she wanted me to betray you again."

"Adric!" Narayan reached out and gripped my arm, above the elbow, until I cried out with the pain of that steely grip and wrenched away, rubbing bruised flesh.

"Sorry," Narayan muttered, looking at his hands, "I forgot I was—" he swallowed, staring at me. "But why do you say—to betray me again? What betrayal? Adric, it was your hand that freed me! Zandru's hells, Adric," he begged, "Adric, *how much have you forgotten? Who and what do you think I am?*"

CHAPTER SEVEN

THE FIRE IN the other room had burned to an ember. Without a glance my way, Narayan mended the fire, sat down, his legs stretched to the little blaze, his chin in his hands, waiting. I could not stand still; I walked, restless, around the room, speaking in little jerks and half-sentences, not knowing how much was memory and how much was what I could piece together from the jigsaw puzzle of this strange, nightmare world.

"You are—you were the Dreamer," I said. "I remember—being bound to you, and later I—I remember when I freed you. Not knowing what it might mean, not knowing whether you might have slain me on the ground of sacrifice."

"No." Narayan was as motionless as Gamine's veils. "No, Adric, never that. We cannot kill one another, you and I. I could order you killed, I suppose, but I—I would never do that unless there was no other way. I always hoped there would be another way, for me, for you."

I tried to trim my words carefully between the two personalities that were battling in my brain. At least I was beginning to reconstruct Adric's story with some coherence and logic, not the isolated scraps I had deduced before.

"Adric freed you," I said. "I am not sure whether it

was for your sake, or whether he wished to—to work for his own power against the others in Rainbow City." Yes, that was the burning incongruity; that Adric, this harsh and cruel man, should have freed a Dreamer, should have worked against his own people and his own power. Why, why? If I knew that, I would have the key to everything.

But I did not know. I sighed and went on.

"Karamy took Adric from you, by treachery," I said. "She sent him, half-mad, back to the Crimson Tower. Karamy's magic stripped him of his memories, broke the bond between you and Adric."

"Not entirely," Narayan said, staring into the fire. "I knew when you woke. But I could not come, myself, into Rainbow City and rescue you. You know what is kept there."

I didn't, but it hardly seemed important now.

"Karamy stripped Adric of memory and power, sent him back to stargazing in Narabedla; she hoped, when at last she let him return, that he would be the old Adric. Karamy needed his power, more than she feared it. But it was not Karamy—" the voice that was not quite mine shook, suddenly, with my own weariness and the blank terror I'd been keeping at bay, "it wasn't Karamy who sent *me* here! I'm not Adric, you were perfectly right, I'm no more Adric than you are! I'm in Adric's body, yes, I have—I have some of his memories, his thoughts, he sometimes moves me like a puppet, but her—" my voice cracked suddenly; I knew I sounded like a hysterical kid, but I couldn't stop once it had broken loose. "I'm not Adric! I'm not, I don't belong here at all."

Narayan jumped up and I heard his hurrying steps behind me; then his steely hands were on my shoulders hard, swinging me around to face him. "All right," he said, "steady. It's all right now."

I drew a long breath and let it out again, shamed. Narayan looked at me, his eyes still skeptical, but he sighed. I could guess his thoughts; *had he broken me down into honesty, or was this more of Adric's treachery?*

I felt a light hand, a leaf-touch, on my arm; then Cynara was holding my hand, looking intently up into my face. "I knew," she whispered. "I couldn't be sure, but once I saw your eyes looking out at me from Adric's face."

I saw the doubt dissolve in Narayan's face. Slowly, he nodded. "I sensed you weren't the Adric I knew," he said. "But I couldn't believe that Adric, when it came to the test, would do that to me. I suppose, for him, it was the easy way out. A perfect way of escape."

He sank down on the bench again, dropping his head into his hands. "A perfect way out," he repeated, and his voice sounded suddenly old and tired. "Let his memories disintegrate, or step into another world, and leave another man in his place. Another personality. And just not care what happened."

I shook my head, still feeling the trembling inside. "But what would Adric want with *my* life?" He was a lord, a powerful warlock; *could* he step into the world of Mike Kenscott, radioman, ordinary citizen of an ordinary world?

"It was a way to escape the trouble he caused," said Cynara, bitterly. "So it was all for nothing! We haven't got Adric, and we've involved an innocent outsider!"

After a long time, Narayan looked up. "That's right;

you're an outsider," he said slowly. "You owe us nothing. But my men think you are Adric, and they think you've been rescued from Karamy, and brought back to us. I'd never be able to convince them otherwise. Do you think *you* could, in Adric's body?"

Cynara answered, clutching my hand in that close, protective way, "They'd think it was more of Karamy's magic. Like—like her zombies. They'd—they'd tear him to pieces, Narayan!"

Narayan said, troubled, "You don't owe us anything. But would you mind pretending to be Adric for a little while longer? Otherwise—" he stopped. I realized that he was not a man who would enjoy making threats, but I could understand his situation. I was just an outsider who messed things up by being, at the same time, Adric.

Well, I seemed to be stuck with it. I certainly didn't feel any loyalty to the Narabedlans of Rainbow City, or give a hang what happened to them. Narayan, by comparison, looked pretty decent. Even if he was making a pretty desperate effort to overthrow the government by force and violence, I couldn't blame him.

In fact, I wouldn't mind helping! I had a few scores to settle with Rainbow City, myself. . . .

And, all these principles aside, it looked like the only way to save my skin—even if it was Adric's skin.

"All right," I said, "I'll try, but what's this all about, anyhow?"

"That's right, you wouldn't know. You have some of Adric's memories, but not all. Do you remember who I am?"

"Not entirely," I said. I remembered—in that strange Adric-way—some things. Narayan had been born, about thirty years before, into a respectable country family who were appalled to realize that they had given birth to one of the mutant Dreamers, and were only too glad to hand him over to those in power at Rainbow City. Still a child, he had been bound into the enforced stasis in the Dreamer's Keep, and there he had slept. ...

Cynara said, "You remember the old Dreamer who served the Crimson Tower?"

I remembered that, too—or Adric did. He had grown old and weak, mortal. He could no longer give, to Adric's vaulting ambition, the full measure of power that Adric had come to desire. And at last he had been eliminated. I bowed my head.

"I slept in the Dreamer's Keep," Narayan said, quietly. "I was awakened and bound to you, and given sacrifice. I learned to use my power, and to give it up to Adric." A brooding horror dwelt in the gray eyes; I realized that Narayan lived in his own personal, private hell with the memory of what he had done under the spell of Narabedla. "Adric was strong."

Yes. Adric had called upon the young Dreamer's developing powers, without counting the cost. What wonder if the memory maddened Narayan? The young Dreamer finally seemed to win his silent struggle for self-control, and went on quietly;

"Well, one day you—or rather, Adric—freed me. I was never sure why. I suppose it was in a moment of remorse." Cynara stirred, but Narayan went on, not seeming to see her.

"I found my sister again, Cynara." And now he raised his eyes to the girl, laying his hand on her shoulder; she smiled, and again I saw the strange protectiveness in that smile, as Narayan said quietly, "I was like a child. I had to learn to live again, all the simplest things. Just being alive took all my strength for months. I was wholly powerless, because I had been trained to use my powers only through the Sacrifice. And I had to learn to—to live without that. It wasn't easy."

"Why?" I asked thoughtlessly.

Narayan's eyes froze me, but his answer dropped the last link into the chain of memory. "To use that power," he said,

Outside the door I could hear the noises of the camp; the light of their watch-fires crept in through the cracks. The fire had burned low again, and Narayan's face was in shadow; he moved restlessly in the dim firelight.

"I have harnessed the power, somewhat," he said. "I can use it myself, a little. For simple things, and to protect myself."

I was beginning, vaguely, to understand. In my own world I had heard of psi powers, of extra-sensory perception, of seance mediums who could do things called magical to those who did not understand them. I had also heard that these wild talents were physically exhausting, draining the physical energy; the collapse of a medium after a seance—I had thought it was fakery. Evidently the Narabedlans had found out a way to harness that psi power, to control it, to provide the energy for increasing it vastly, by feeding the Dreamers on the life energy of living men. ...

I shuddered, a bone-deep, racking thing that left me weak and white, and dropped nerveless on the seat. Cynara held me tight.

"No," said Narayan grimly, watching my face, "it's not pretty. But if I had any doubts of your not being

Adric that would have finished them. You really didn't know, did you?"

I shook my head, still sick with the horror of it.

"Well, I learned to live without it," said Narayan, his face quiet and controlled again. "Then Cynara was taken for sacrifice." His eyes on the girl were tender. "Adric freed her, redeemed her, gave her the freedom of Rainbow City. He could do that because Evarin was weak and Gamine did not care. Even the Lords of the Rainbow have many commoners in their retinue. Not a spy there, never that. But someone to act as a link between us, Adric and me. Then there was Rhys, the old Dreamer."

Rhys. The only Dreamer-mutant ever born within Rainbow City.

"Yes. Gamine is bound to Rhys, but is careless and lets him wake for long periods of time, and Rhys and I have been in contact. I hardly know how to explain this to anyone else, our minds can speak."

"Telepathy too?" I murmured.

"Only to another Dreamer. He helped me to learn to use my powers. But he will not raise a hand against Narabedla. They are his kindred too."

I was hearing scraps of conversation from a vast abyss of time and space, whence I had been drawn in electrical coma across the Time Ellipse. *They will know, Narayan will know.* And Adric; *What have I to do with Narayan?* Adric had been playing a fancy double game with Narayan, and I opened my mouth to say so, but the young Dreamer was still talking, and I lost track of the words, thinking of Rhys.

Perhaps this was why Rhys had helped Adric find a way out of his world, because it had helped Rhys, too, find an escape from an unbearable conflict. With

Adric gone, Rhys need not face a choice between his kindred in Narabedla, and his wish to see the Dreamers freed. With Adric gone, perhaps the old, old man could live out his last few years in a world precariously at peace.

"I had forgotten, we had all forgotten, that Adric was Narabedlan too. Until he vanished, until Karamy stretched out her hand and took him back." Narayan's voice brooded. These men had been friends.

"Adric was gone, and the hand of Narabedla lay heavy on us. Without Adric to lead them we felt there was a chance for rebellion. I have been working, planning—you saw." He bit his lip. "Then I knew that Adric was free, and I sent Brennan to see why he did not return to us. Brennan didn't come back."

I lowered my head and miserably told him what had happened to Brennan.

Narayan's face looked haggard in the firelight. "He was a brave man," Narayan said at last. "He knew what he faced, and dared it. I don't blame you. After the change, there was a time when you went on living Adric's life, almost by reflex, thinking his thoughts, carrying out his habits. But now he will grow weaker in you, I think. I *hope*. Who are you in your own world?"

He thought Adric would grow weaker in me. I had feared that Adric would grow stronger and stronger, until he crowded me out entirely. Was Narayan right? Was Adric gone for good? "My name is Mike Kenscott," I said at last. "Michael."

"Michael." Cynara turned the strange word on her tongue, curiously. Her hand, forgotten, still lay in mine. "And what are you? A great lord of magic?"

I laughed, wearily; cut off the laughter as I looked into the lovely face. "No, girl," I said softly, "there's no magic in my world." *Magic?* I'd have to think about that.

"It must be very strange," she murmured, "strange and a little frightening, to change worlds. I can remember Narayan when he came from the Dreamer's Keep, with a life to learn."

Was it only compassion in her dark eyes, compassion for a man suffering the same disorientation as the brother she had cherished and protected? Or was it something more? "Michael," she repeated softly.

Narayan broke into our natural absorption, gently. "The men will have to call you Adric; they will believe you are Adric come back to us. Later, perhaps—" he shrugged. I didn't say anything. I was still afraid I hadn't seen the last of Adric; but I liked this man. And Cynara, clinging to my hand, the one person in this world who had known and accepted me for *myself*, not as a shadow of Adric.

Narayan moved to turn on lights. "It's very late," he said, "and you must be worn out. We've taught even the Narabedlans to stay out of the forests by night, lately, so we're safe enough here, even if they had some idea of getting Adric back. And in any case, they can't do much until they've been to the Dreamer's Keep. If we can cut them off from the source of their magic—" he smiled, and with a sudden, boyish friendliness he held out his hand. "Well tomorrow we'll see what comes! Michael—" he hesitated, then said, almost reluctant to speak the words, "I'm glad you're not Adric. He might be hard to handle, now."

As if the lights had been a signal—for all I knew,

they were—Raif came back into the room without knocking. Narayan crossed his hostile stare at me. "It's all right, Raif," he said. "Adric has come back to us."

The elephantine face creased up in a sudden grin. "I'm sorry I handled you so roughly, Lord Adric. But I had orders, and I wasn't sure."

"I'd have done the same thing myself," I said, and took the hand he offered.

"Find him a place to sleep," Narayan suggested, and, with a backward glance at Cynara, I followed Raif up a low flight of the farmhouse stairs into an empty room. There was a bed there, clean but rumpled; Raif said "Kerrel went on watch at the roadway; he won't be back much before noon. You can sleep here."

I kicked off my boots and crawled between the blankets, suddenly too weary to speak. I had been two days without sleep, and most of that time I had been under exhausting physical and mental strain, in two worlds. I saw Raif cautiously finger his weapon, and sensed that whatever Narayan said, he wasn't taking too many chances with Adric. I didn't blame him. He had brains, this outsize lieutenant of Narayan's.

Sleepily I said "You can put that away, friend elephant. I'm not even going to move until I've had a good, long—"

I didn't even finish the sentence. I went to sleep.

I had slept for hours. I came out of confused dreams—a great wheeling bird, a knife, Andy's face, the blue blur of Gamine's veiling, the pitiful cry of a woman in anguish—when I heard a softer voice, and felt small hands pulling me upright. I opened my eyes to see Cynara's dark lovely eyes gazing down at me.

"Michael, wake up! Karamy and Evarin are riding today, hunting Adric! Hunting you!"

I sat up, dizzy-brained, far from alert, still stupid with sleep; I could not understand her agitation, or the way she had spoken to me. But I put a careless, reassuring arm around her shoulders for a moment. Then, hearing the swift noise of steps on the stairs, released her, bent and began to pull on my boots.

Narayan shoved open the door, dragging a brown tunic over his head as he came. "I see Cynara's told you the news," he said. "I was right. We'll have to move quickly now. If they have too good hunting—"

He fumbled with the laces of his shirt. A dead weariness was in his eyes; they looked flat, almost glazed. He met my questioning stare and smiled tiredly.

"The Dreamers stir," he told me. "I am not yet free of that need, not wholly. So I must be careful."

Cynara shuddered and threw her arms around her brother's neck, clutching him in a fiercely sheltering clasp. But he was already deep in thought again; he freed her arms without impatience. "We'll meet that when the time comes, little sister. So Karamy and Evarin ride hunting, Idris too, most like." His brows contracted. "All but Gamine," he mused. "If I could only get through to Rhys." Then, with an impatient gesture, he put the thought aside. "I don't dare. Not with *that* stirring."

I understood. Narayan was still attuned to the terrible hungers of the sleeping Dreamers in the Keep. Well, that was to be expected.

As for me, I felt fresh and strong, and my mind was

working again, though with some strange blurs. How had I come here to the house of the freed Dreamer? Just what had happened last night? I had thought Narayan would never trust me again, but now, when I needed it most, here I was in his complete confidence again.

Soft fool!

Yes, this was better than any of Karamy's plans! Damn Karamy anyhow, meddling with my memory, but at least it had served my turn last night, to step aside into another identity, win Narayan's confidence!

And Karamy had the audacity to fly Evarin's devilbirds after me? After *me*, Adric of the Crimson Tower? Well, she should have a lesson she would never forget—and so should the damned Toymaker himself —and so should this walking zombie here, staring stupidly at me with a foolish smile of friendship. Gods of the Rainbow, what preposterous things had I done and said last night?

"Let them come, birds and all," I said. "There's been no Sacrifice for some time. They have no other resources." I laughed soundlessly at the thought; *are you short on magic today, Karamy? Forced to use the foolish gimcracks of the Toymaker?* "We'll take them tonight at the Dreamer's Keep."

But what you do not know, Narayan, I added to myself with secret satisfaction, *is that you will join them there! When I have used your powers in my revenge against those who were leagued against me, then you will go back to your place, Dreamer! Till then, plan to crush me and mine! Dream on—dream your waking dreams, till I scatter them. . . .*

It never occurred to the soft fool to question if the

Adric of last night were the Adric of this morning. We went downstairs and snatched a quick breakfast. Cynara saw the winged, flame-colored cloak she had worn in Rainbow City, lying on the settle, snatched it up wrathfully and stuffed it into the fireplace. In her plain gray dress, her shy prettiness was more striking than ever. Cynara was not Karamy, but she was a pretty thing, and after all, it helped Narayan to trust me when Cynara perched on the arm of my chair and ran her dainty fingers over the bruises on my face.

"Your roughnecks nearly killed him, Narayan!"

"Oh, I'm not hurt." I made my voice gentle for her ears alone. But I scowled darkly into my plate, pushed the food away and strode out into the camp. Narayan shouted quickly, jumping up, sending his chair crashing backward, as he ran after me and we went down the steps together. "Wait, wait! Don't forget, to them, you're still a traitor," he commanded.

I kept my voice foolish and humble. "I had forgotten."

"I know the truth, and they'll take my word," Narayan said with his friendly smile. He took my arm, and we walked like that through the tents, Narayan's expression almost belligerent. I saw the faces of the men as they came out of their rude shelters, saw suspicion and mistrust giving way to tolerance and then to acceptance and relaxation as they watched us walking arm in arm. Finally Narayan called to Raif, "Watch him, will you? Some of the men may not know yet."

"There's not much time for this nonsense," I said. "If they're out hunting. Raif, find me twelve men who aren't afraid to come close to Rainbow City."

Raif glanced at Narayan, who looked surprised. Then Narayan said, "I give what orders you want, Adric," and I had to hide a smile. Before long I would win back the place my foolishness had lost! The idiot whose body I had shared briefly had almost put it beyond redemption, but in a way he had helped, too; he had won Narayan's trust as I could never have done. Well, that futile booby should not share in my coming triumph! Nor should Narayan.

Fumbling in my pocket, I touched something hard and smooth. Evarin's magic mirror, not true magic but the product of his childish tinkering. Still, it might serve. Narayan looked over my shoulder curiously as I pulled it out. "What is that?"

"One of Evarin's Toys. I may find a use for it," I said, and tossed it idly to him. "Look at it, if you like." I held my breath; Narayan took it in his hand for a moment, curiously, but did not untwist the silk. "Go ahead," I urged, "unwrap it."

I might have sounded too eager; abruptly, Narayan handed it back. "Here. You'd better keep it. I don't know anything about Evarin."

I should have known it would not be that easy. Feigning indifference, I thrust it back into my pocket. It didn't matter one way or another, Narayan would lose. For Evarin and Karamy rode a-hunting today, and I knew what their game would be.

CHAPTER EIGHT

I PULLED MY cloak closer about me, prickling with excitement, as I knelt between Raif and Kerrel in the tree-platform. Just beneath me, Narayan clung to a lower branch. My ears picked up the ring of distant hoofbeats on the frozen ground, and I smiled.

I knew every nuance of this hunt. Evarin might not find his birds so obedient to his call today! A scrap of me remembered another world, where a dazed and bewildered other self had flown at a living bird with his pocketknife, and I spared a moment to laugh at the memory.

Boldly, I plotted possibilities. There must be a snare. But who? Narayan himself? No, he was my only protection until I could get free of this riffraff. Besides, he said he had been learning to use his power—unaided. If he unleased it, at close range like this, he could drain me lifeless, as a spider sucks a trapped fly.

Kerrel then, or Raif. I had a grudge against the fat man, anyhow.

I plucked at Raif's sleeve. "Wait here for me," I said, cunningly, and made as if to leave the platform. Raif walked smiling into the trap. "Here, Adric! Narayan gave orders you weren't to run into any danger! After all! it's you they want!"

Good, good! I didn't even have to order the man to his death; he volunteered. "Well, we want a scout out," I demurred, "to carry word when they come." *As if we wouldn't know!*

"I'll go." Raif leaned past me, touching Narayan's shoulder. He explained in a whisper—we were all whispering, though there was no need for it—and Narayan nodded. "But don't show yourself."

I held back laughter. *As if that would matter!*

The man swung down into the road. I heard his heavy tread strike rock; heard footsteps diminish, die in the distance; felt it, like a tangible prickling of the nerves, when he passed the limit of Narayan's perceptions. *Yes, we were still bound, like an invisible net! If I could only read his thoughts . . . but no. Then he'd be able to read mine!*

A clamoring, bestial cry ripped the air, a cry that seemed to ring and echo up out of hell, a cry no human throat could compass. But I knew what had screamed. That settled the fat man! Narayan jerked all over, his blonde face white as death. "Raif!" The word was almost a prayer.

We half-scrambled, half-leaped into the road. Side by side, we ran down the roadway together.

The screaming of a bird warned me. I looked up and dodged quickly. Over my head a great scarlet falcon, wide-winged, wheeled and darted in at me. Narayan's yell cut the air; I ducked, flinging up a fold of my cloak over my head. I ripped the knife from my belt and slashed upward, ducking my head, keeping one arm over my eyes. The bird wavered, hung in the air, watching me with live green eyes that shifted with every movement. The falcon's trappings were green, bright against the scarlet feathers.

I knew who had flown this bird!

The falcon wheeled, banking like a plane, and rushed in again. Falcon? But no egg had hatched these birds, and I knew who had shaped these scarlet pinions!

From behind my cloak-wrapped arm I saw Narayan pull the pistol-like electro-rod, and screamed warning:

"Drop it. Quick!"

The bird, holding Evarin's powers at this moment, could turn gunfire as easily as Evarin himself; could absorb the energy and in turn be re-charged by it. And if the falcon drew a drop of my blood, then I was slave to whoever had flown it.

I thrust upward with the knife, dodging between the bird's wings. Men leaped toward us, knives out and ready. The bird screamed wildly, flew upward a little way, and hovered, watching us with those curiously intelligent green eyes. Another falcon, and another, winged across the road, and a thin uncanny screeching echoed in the city air. I heard a tinny jingle of little bells. The three birds—golden- and green-trapped and harnessed in royal purple—swung above us; three pairs of unwinking jewel eyes hung motionless in a row. And far behind us, against the darkening sky at the horizon, the dropping red sun silhouetted three figures, on horses, motionless there; Evarin, Idris and Karamy, intent on the falcon-play, three traitors baiting the one who had escaped their hands.

For a moment, briefly, I wished I were on the other side of this hunt. Slaves we had in plenty, but the taking of passive victims is dull stuff, and ai, the falcon-game was good sport! Body left behind, all senses poured into the stuff of the bird, soaring and darting down upon the terrified victim, playing with him as an eagle plays with her helpless prey! Darting at the eyes, the tender parts, thrusting, drawing the blood that gave power over him, watching the helpless terror of the victim. Or, at times—but how rarely!—a spirited fight against some victim made bold by despair. A dangerous game, for if he killed the bird, it was a painful and nasty shock. But what is a game without danger? There were always more birds. And the victim who escaped your hands once could be taken and tormented at leisure.

And I had faced the falcons before this, too; flown, myself, against another for a wager, or pitted myself, armed only with a knife, against another's bird. But this was no rough game with my kindred for careless sport or light stakes. This was deadly in earnest; they had all massed themselves against me, and I'd need every scrap of skill.

The falcons hung, poised, swept inward in massed attack. They darted between my knife and Narayan's; behind me a fearful scream rang out, and I knew one of the falcons, at least, had drawn blood; that one of the men behind us was not ours! Turning and stumbling, the stricken man ran blindly through the clearing, down the road; tripped, reeled, stumbled over the body of a man who lay across the roadway under his feet. Narayan gave a gasping, retching sound, and I whirled in time to see him jerk out his electro-rod and fire shot after wild shot at the stumbling figure that had been our man.

"Fire!" he panted to me. "Larno wouldn't want to—to get to them. He'd rather be dead."

I struck down the weapon, savagely. "Fool! Some

hunting they must have!" Narayan began protesting, and I wrenched the rod from him. The man was far beyond firing range now. At Narayan's convulsed face I swore, savagely. This weak fool would ruin everything! What was one man more or less?

I glanced around, orienting myself quickly. The birds hung away again, and I motioned Narayan's men in close. "Don't fire on the birds," I cautioned them. "It only energizes them. They soak up the power from your weapons. Use knives. Cut their wings and try to immobilize them. Look out!" The falcons, like chain-lightning, traced thin orbits down in a flash of color, then darted in, in a slapping confusion of beaks and beating wings. I backed away, flicking up my cloak, beating at the birds with the weighted edge; our men, standing in a close circle, back to back, fought them off with knives and the ends of their cloaks, swatting them away. Three times I heard the inhuman scream, three times I heard the lurching footsteps as a man—not human any more—broke away from us and ran blindly, stumbling toward the distant ridge.

I heard Narayan cry out, whirled to him. He ran toward me, beating back the purple-trapped bird that darted in and out on swift, agile wings. The screeching of the falcons, the flapping of cloaks, the hoarse breathing of men hard-pressed, gave the whole scene a nightmarish unreality in which the only real thing was Narayan fighting at my side. His gasp made me whirl by instinct, flinging up my cloak to protect my back; my knife thrust out to cover his throat. He raked a long gash across the falcon's head above the beak, was rewarded with a scream of unbirdlike agony and the spasmodic open-and-shut convulsing of the talons. They razored outclawing. They furrowed a slash in the Dreamer's arm. The deadly beak darted in to cut, but I threw myself forward, unprotected, off balance, ready to strike.

At the last moment, talons and beak drew back from Narayan, turned aside straight for me, with more than birdlike intelligence! And my knife was turned aside guarding Narayan!

But Narayan jerked aside. His knife fell unheeded in the road as his arms shot out and grabbed the bird behind the head, twisting his whole body convulsively to be out of range of the stabbing needle of beak. The bird lunged, pecking at the cloak that wrapped his forearm. Thrown off balance, I stumbled against Narayan and we fell together in a tangle of cloaks and knives and thrashing, slapping wings, asprawl in the road. The wings beat like a cyclone, the cruel talons, thrust with the power of steel, raked my face and Narayan's, but Narayan hung on grimly, holding the deadly beak away. I fumbled, blinded by the wings slapping against his face, for the knife; thrust again and again. Thin yellow blood spouted in great gouts, splattering us both with burning venom.

I snatched the struggling bird from the Dreamer's weakening hands and twisted until I heard the neck snap in my fingers. The bird's wild struggles suddenly stopped; it went limp between my hands. Whatever had given it life had withdrawn.

And high on the ridge above us the dwarfed figure of Idris threw up his hands and collapsed like an empty sack across the pommel of his saddle.

Narayan's breath went out in a long, limp sigh as we untangled our twisted bodies from one another and the dead falcon. Our eyes met briefly as we mopped away the blood, and he smiled, shakily, spontaneously. Damn it, what a waste! I liked this man! Almost I wished I need not send him back to tranced and horrible dreams.

He said quietly "There is a life between us now."

I twisted my face into a smile matching his. "That's one of them," I said savagely, turned to watch the other two falcons tearing into the ring of men. "Come on," Narayan shouted, and he flung ourselves into the breach. I threw down my knife, snatched a sword from somebody, and waded in, swinging the sword in great arcs that seemed somehow right and natural. The men scattered before the sword, like scared chickens. The falcons dipped down; I went berserk with hate, sweeping it in vicious semicircles against the lashing birds.

The sword cut empty air and I realized, blankly, that both birds lay cut to ribbons at my feet. Their yellow blood washed the dead leaves. Narayan's eyes swam through a red haze into my field of vision. They were watching me, trouble and fright in their gray depths. I forced myself to sanity and dropped the sword on the dead birds.

"That's that," I said briefly.

We took toll of our losses. Three, four men, lost to the slavery of the birds. Most of the rest had razor-slashes from the talons, and Narayan, gasping with pain, rubbed a spot of the yellow blood from his face. "That stuff burns!" he grimaced. I laughed, tightly. He didn't have to tell me. We'd both have festered burns, deep as the brand of red-hot iron, to deal with tomorrow; the stuff Evarin used for the "blood" of his birds was deadly.

"You saved my life." Narayan's voice was quiet,

and I bit my lip against murderous rage. Fool that I was, why hadn't I stood back? The Dreamers are invulnerable to ordinary human attacks, but they can be put out of action—

And yet I had acted without thinking, to save Narayan. Was there such a bond between us? I found myself shaking with doubt.

"Are you hurt?" Narayan asked. "Let me see your arm," but I shoved him away. Savagely, I told myself not to be a fool. Of course I had protected Narayan. I needed him still, and I wanted him strong and unharmed; nothing as quick and simple as an easy death. He'd rather die than go back to the Dreamer's Keep; I felt sure of that. Well, he wasn't going to be given a choice.

"Look!" One of the men stared, pointed upward, his face tense with fright. Another great bird of prey hung balanced on the wind above us; but as we watched, it wheeled and swiftly winged toward the Rainbow City. One of the men was quickly nocking an arrow to the bow, but the bird was too far and too high; I could barely see the azure shimmer of the bells and harness. A thin sweet tinkling came from them, like a mocking echo of the spell-singer's voice.

Gamine!

CHAPTER NINE

Back in the windowless house, we snatched a hurried meal, cared for our slashes and burns, and tried to plan further. The others had not been idle while I led a picked party against the falcons. All day Narayan's vaunted army had been accumulating—I could hardly say assembling—in the great bowl of land between Rainbow City and the Dreamer's Keep.

There were, perhaps, four thousand men, armed with clumsy powder weapons, not more than half a hundred of the electro-rods like Narayan's, with worn swords that looked as if they had been long buried, with pitchforks, with scythes, even with knobbed wooden clubs. I was put to it to conceal my contempt for this ragtag and bobtail of an army. And Narayan proposed to storm the might of Narabedla, the magical powers of Rainbow City with this?

Yet everywhere I saw looks, heard scraps of conversation, cries and salutes, showing me the confidence that these desperate men had in their leader. Were they all mad, or deluded? *So much the better*, I thought grimly. *Take him from them, and they'll scatter to their rat-holes again!*

I felt my lips twisting in a bitter smile. They trusted Adric, too—Adric, who had freed the Dreamer. When I had shown myself to them, their shouts had made the very trees echo. Well—again the ironic smile came, unbidden—that was just as well too. When Narayan was properly reprisoned, I could use the power of their lost leader to tear down what he himself had built. The thought was deliciously funny.

"What are you laughing about?" Narayan asked me. We were lounging on the steps of the house, watching the men thronging around the camp. His slumberous gray eyes held deep sparks of fire, and without waiting for my answer, he went on, "Think of it! The curse of the Dreamers' magic lifted from this land. The tyranny of the Rainbow Cities gone forever. Think what it means! It means life and hope for any number of people, with no more fear, no more slavery, no sacrifices and raids, no evil birds—" he broke off, spreading his hands in a helpless gesture. "But you can't know. Even with all of Adric's memories, you couldn't know!"

I remembered that he thought I was still Michael Kenscott. Dimly, like something in a dream, I could remember Michael's loyalty for Narayan. *They were two of a kind, fools, soft weaklings.* . . .

And even more dimly I could remember when I had shared that dream, when it had seemed more worthy than the lust for power. Cynara came down the steps and bent to me, laying her soft arm around my shoulder, and I drew her down, but a volcano of hate, so great that I had to hide my face, burned up in me. This man Narayan was my equal—no, I admitted it grudgingly, my superior—and I hated him for it. I hated him because he could not be killed save by mischance, and because he risked that invulnerable state in a way I would never have dared, even in the days when I had been guarded by all his magic. I hated him because I knew that in his dream of power no one would suffer, and I hated him because I knew what I would do with his powers, once I had him safely bound in the Dreamer's Keep again, fed with the energy that would force him to give them up piecemeal to me. And above all, I hated him because once I had been weak enough to share his dream.

"You said once there was no magic in your world, Michael," Narayan broke into my thoughts, and I started. Well, let him deceive himself! I shrugged. "I suppose you'd call the forces of my world magical enough, until you understood them," I temporized.

"The falcon-hunt—Adric told me once that if the falcon was destroyed, the one who was inhabiting it went into shock," Narayan said musingly. "That means Idris, Evarin, Karamy, all three of them out of action for a time. If we could strike right away—"

I said abruptly, "Your plans are good, Narayan. There's just one thing wrong with them; they won't work. Storming Rainbow City won't get you anywhere. It won't even make a beginning. You could kill Karamy's slaves by the hundreds, or the thousands, or the millions, but you couldn't kill Karamy. And the more slaves you kill, the more she'll search out and enslave to replace them. You've got to strike at them in the Dreamer's Keep. It's the only place they're vulnerable."

He did not question my knowledge, or Adric's memories. It was Cynara who reminded me, "Narayan's freedom is limited, remember. He cannot go into Rainbow City, or to the Dreamer's Keep, because Adric, freeing him, could not locate his talisman."

Narayan nodded. "So I've no choice. I'll have to attack them on the road to the Keep, and take my chances."

"What's your army for?" I asked, rudely, "to knock down haycocks? The army can deal with the guards, and the slaves, but the Narabedlans have to be taken in the Dreamer's Keep; it's the only way. I'll go to Rainbow City for you, and get the thing!"

"You?" Narayan and Cynara turned on me, simultaneously, and I reminded myself not to seem too confident; it was Kenscott's display of weakness that had made Narayan trust him. But Cynara's eyes were glowing. "Yes, and I'll go too, in case your memories fail."

Good, good and better. That suited me perfectly! Rainbow City was empty except for old Rhys, and perhaps Gamine, who had not flown falcon with the others, and was presumably indifferent to the internal struggles of the other Narabedlans. But Narayan looked doubtful. "Adric tried that once," he said sombrely, "and all that happened was Karamy recaptured him, and sent him out on the Time Ellipse."

"But Karamy won't be here this time; she and the others will be busy with your army," I reminded him. It was settled that way, and I listened to their plans and suggestions, half contemptuously. Yes, the Narabedlans were vulnerable in the Dreamer's Keep, but if I were there, with Narayan, and Narayan's talisman in my hands, I could stop worrying about Evarin, Idris and the rest.

Cynara bent lightly to touch the ripped talon-mark across my face. "You're hurt again, and you never told me," she accused. "Come this minute and let me take care of it!"

I almost laughed. Me, Adric of the Crimson Tower, being ordered around by a little country girl! I snorted, but spoke pleasantly.

"I'll live, I expect. Come and sit here with us." I pulled her down at my side, but she leaned her head against her brother's knee, and her face was troubled.

She was a pretty thing, and I thought, watching her, that I could forgive her, almost, for being the cause of all my troubles. When I took the girl, for a whim, from among Karamy's slaves, I had not known she was Narayan's sister. And then—and then —like a live wire jolting in my brain, the flash and the blankness. *What lay hidden there? What had I forgotten?* I put my two fists to my temples, as if to tear out the memory by main force, but nothing came except the blur of a face—blonde like Narayan's, white with terror—and a voice speaking words I could not understand, the silvery-sweet voice of Gamine. *Who, what was Gamine?*

"Michael—" Cynara looked frightened, and I brought myself back, by main force, to the present. I made myself smile.

"You—looked so fierce, so far away," she said, faltering, "like—like Adric, not like *you*."

I reached out to draw her to me, but she pulled away, rising lightly to her feet, like a dove poised for flight. I raised her slim fingers to my lips for a moment before I freed her. The gesture pleased her, so much that I watched with contempt as she tripped away. Silly, simple girl! It would please her!

The white sun, incandescent on the horizon, was still bright enough to blur the red sun to a pale spot, when we set out for Rainbow City. Cynara rode at my side; Narayan was to come a part of the way. Kerrel had taken the army, in sections, to set an ambush for Karamy's guard near the Dreamer's Keep; I listened to Narayan giving him instructions, to the sound of grief in his voice when he spoke Raif's name.

But at last we took the opposite road, a winding, twisting road that led through the forested country to Rainbow City. Cynara rode beside me, her dark eyes brilliant, her cheeks red with the cold, lovely in her gray dress, but it did not suit her as the winged, flame-colored cloak of Narabedla had suited her. There was dainty witchery in Cynara, and a pretty trust that made me smile and promise, recklessly, "We will win." It pleased me to think that I could comfort Cynara for her brother's downfall. Once conditioned anew to Rainbow City, she would forget all this, and be a fair and beautiful companion. If she continued to please me. Well, it might be amusing to see this unformed country girl wield all the power of Karamy the Golden!

But would she ever look at me with so much trust again?

I cursed my fancies, savagely, and dug my heels into my horse's flank. What did that matter? Was I morbid or mad again to care for that?

It took us an hour of hard riding to reach the lip of the great cup of land, where we paused, looking down the dark, almost-straight alleyway of trees that led to the walls of Rainbow City. I whistled tunelessly between my teeth.

"Whatever we do, it's going to be wrong," I said. "We'd be taking quite a chance to ride up to the main gate this way. At the same time, they'd be expecting us—if we came at all—to sneak in the back way;

they'd never expect us to ride straight up the front avenue."

"The deer walks safest at the hunter's door," quoted Narayan, laughing, "but won't they be expecting us to use that kind of logic?"

Cynara giggled but stopped at my frown. "At that rate," I said, "we could go on all night."

Narayan reached overhead, snatching down a crackling sheaf of frost-berries, selected one narrow pod. He held it between finger and thumb. "Chance. Two seeds, we go around; three, we ride straight up to the main gate. Agreed?" I nodded, and he crushed the dry husk. One, two, three seeds rolled into my outstretched palm.

"Fate," said Narayan. "Ready?"

I jounced the seeds in my palm. "One for Evarin, and one for Idris, and one for Karamy," I said contemptuously, and flung the little black balls into the road. "We'll scatter them like that."

We were lucky. The drive was deserted; if there were guards out, they had been posted on the secret paths that Adric knew. Straight toward the towers we rode, and just before dusk we checked our horses and tethered them within half a mile of the Rainbow City, going forward cautiously on foot. I objected to this arrangement. "I'll get in alone," I told them. "If anything happens to me, they mustn't lose you as well."

"I can't go inside," Narayan said, "but I'll come as close as I can. If anything goes wrong, well, I'll be here to help."

Silently, I damned the man's loyalty, but there was nothing I could say without spoiling the illusion I had worked so hard to create. I took his hand for a moment. "Thank you."

His voice was equally abrupt. "Good luck."

Cynara moved forward with me; I stopped, glanced at her with a frown.

"I'm coming," she said fiercely, and clung to my hand. "I'm coming, and there's no way you can stop me!"

So much loyalty? For me?

Still, she might be useful, if only as hostage later. "Come on, then," I said, "but keep your wits about you. They'll probably have all the bolt-holes guarded, and I'm not even sure yet how we're going to get in."

"Narayan," she asked, "can you help?"

The young Dreamer's face was in shadow, where we stood under the great dark loom of the outwalls, but I could tell that he was very pale. "Perhaps," he muttered, seeming to force the words out through some strange sluggishness. "I will try. Brennan came this way," he shook his head, as if dizzied.

"Maybe you'd better try," I said cautiously, "I have no magic, remember."

We moved slowly along, keeping in the lee of the rampart; Narayan moved unsteadily, on faltering feet. Then he stumbled; quickly, my hand was on his arm.

"You'd better go back," I said quickly. "We'll find a way in somehow."

I needed Narayan whole and strong, later! Afterward, when he had served my turn—

Cynara was looking at him, trouble in her eyes. He tried to smile reassuringly, but the effort only contracted the muscles of his face. "I don't know—exactly why it is," he said thickly, "I don't know what was done, but as I come closer to the walls I can feel my strength—leaving—me—"

I supported him upright, guiding his steps back away from the outwall. On the surface, I was all solicitude; inwardly I rejoiced. Now I knew what I wanted to know. Not in my lifetime had a freed Dreamer walked in Narabedla, except for old Rhys who was one of us, and my knowledge was hazy; I had not known how close Narayan could come to the forbidden areas.

Long years ago, generations ago, when the Dreamers first threatened the might of Rainbow City, there had been another Toymaker in Narabedla, and he had found the way to bind the Dreamers. They could not be killed. But he had made, and set up in Rainbow City, a device—blurred, vague memories of Mike Kenscott's world flickered across my consciousness, with words like *vibrations,* and *subsonics*— which, harmless to everyone else, worked selectively on the Dreamers who had been bound to Narabedla. A similar device, in the Dreamer's Keep, held them bound in their tranced sleep. Still a child, each of the mutant Dreamers we brought into contact with this device, and bound into rapport with one of the Narabedlans, as Narayan to me.

The effects of this device could be nullified, for brief periods of time, by the talismans. The Narabedlan kept the talisman (magic? vibrations?) that would wake his Dreamer and at the time of the sacrifice, the Dreamer was waked; fed with the life-energy that increased his powers tenfold, and these powers transferred to the giver of the sacrifice.

Magic?

Narayan brushed a hand across his eyes. "I'm all right here," he told me. "But until you get my talisman, this is about as close as I can come."

Did he really think I would turn it over to him? Yes, I supposed he was that foolish, to think that Adric, having given him his freedom, would also make him free of Rainbow City and the Dreamer's Keep—to destroy us all!

Cynara looked back at Narayan, uneasily, as we approached the outwalls again. But my attention was turned to the problem of getting in. I looked up at the ramparts of the outwall, surrounding the great semicircle of towers that was Rainbow City, their iridescent shine blurred to a dark glow in the dying sunlight. Rainbow City, a city no longer. Old, half-blurred memories nagged at me; there had been a day when this great castle had been alive with men and women, filled to the brim with joyous bustle, sport, and happiness—not the eerie, half-deserted haunt of half a dozen surviving warlocks of my caste, with their zombie retinue of the living dead! Cynara's hand felt warm in mine, and I felt that for a moment she almost shared my thoughts.

"It could be so beautiful."

"It will be beautiful again," I promised, "but just now we have to get in."

Around an angle of the ramparts there was a gate, little known, perhaps unguarded. We approached it fearfully, expecting every moment to hear a challenge or feel a bolt out of darkness; stole closer, keeping in the lee of the rampart.

The gate was open.

It swung, ajar, on hinges that creaked softly, rhythmically back and forth. Beyond it was darkness. I swept Cynara back with one arm, staring with hard eyes at that darkness. "Careful," I muttered, "it could be a trap."

And I had no magic! Carefully, on tiptoe, I stole closer to the gate.

Still nothing but the silent creaking. I beckoned with one arm, stepping through. Cynara followed me, her light footsteps sounding loud in the echoing stillness.

We were inside Rainbow City.

We stood in a pillared court, long and narrow, alabaster flagstones under foot, a long dark passageway opening before us, a dim patch of sunset sky high overhead. At one end of the court was a curved high-rising wall, shimmering greenly, the Emerald Tower, and at the other end, the pale loom of the Azure Tower rose blue and high over us. The colors were dimmed with dusk, and our very breathing seemed to give back echoes. I stood, looking around, trying to orient myself. The walls of the court cut off any view of the other towers, and as always, when I tried to concentrate on any one detail it grew vague in my mind.

Cynara flinched and cried out as a shadow crossed us; I whirled, my breath coming loud, my hand already dragging my sword from the sheath. High above us a falcon wheeled, spiraled down; I heard the thin-sweet tinkling of bells. *Gamine!* I thrust Cynara behind me, but the falcon made no move to attack; it hovered, eyes bright with mechanical glitter, pinions moving faintly to sustain it on the high air above us. I clenched my fingers nervously on swordhilt, itching to strike, but it hung out of reach, just watching, and somehow the poise of the wings made me think of the calm, malicious detachment of Gamine. But I kept my hand on my sword, guiding Cynara with one hand into the passageway.

It was wide and high, but seemed cramped after the open court, and I walked warily, glancing over my shoulder to see if the falcon would follow, but it did not. I saw it dart down and veer away again; heard the high screeching and the jingle of bells as it swept upward and vanished from our sight.

I went quickly now, finding my way through the labyrinth toward the Crimson Tower, Cynara hurrying at my side. We crossed open courts with pools and gardens and fountains quickly, keeping in the lee of the buildings, wary of being seen. I knew where I was, now. One more court, and one more passageway ...

Before us, the walls of the Crimson Tower rose at last, shining like a still-burning coal. Low lurid light burned in the courtyard before us; I breathed more freely. Now, at least, I was on familiar ground.

Cynara screamed, and I whirled, sword out and ready. Behind me, advancing in an unbroken line that spanned the court from one side to another, a round dozen of Karamy's guards in their gold and crimson advanced on slow feet; the lurid light sparked red on the steel tips of eight-foot pikes, leveled in a spear-wall toward my breast. In the burning twilight their faces were stolid, expressionless; they called no challenge, seemed to show neither battle-lust nor excitement. They simply advanced, step by mechanical step, pikes extended. Cynara shrank away; I took a step backward, darting my eyes along the line. Hopeless. There was no break in that solid phalanx, that advanced foot by slow foot, relentlessly.

"Quick," I cried, "Cynara! Into the tower!" and gripped my sword, not that I could reach any of them against those long pikes! My eyes darted from side to side, seeking escape. The steel points came closer, closer. ...

Then one of the zombie guards leaped into the air, still horribly silent, clawed at his breast, collapsed and lay still, with a clattering of his pike. I flung the useless sword away, snatched at the fallen guard's pike. Behind me Cynara stood shaking, Narayan's long black electro-rod in her small hands; she was steadying the weapon with both hands, twisting it frantically for another shot.

The zombie guards had neither halted nor hesitated, advancing step by mechanical step, closing the rank of their dead comrade. Gripping the pike, I swung it, knocked two of the oncoming pikes aside, while the guards tottered and fell back. I ran the pike into one man's breast; he writhed horribly, half jerking the weapon from my hands, in that terrible voiceless silence; then died without a groan. I pulled the pike clear, leaped up the steps of the Crimson Tower. Past me, a white bolt crackled and another of the guards leaped, silently clawed his breast, and fell lifeless.

Still in that ghastly silence, the remaining pikesmen milled in confusion. I snatched the electro-rod from Cynara, my fingers manipulating the controls with swift skill; swept it into the ranks. The guards, half their number lying dead, ran aimlessly back and forth, pikes thrusting mindlessly into the air, as if at some silent signal, then turned and silently fled, the sound of their booted feet dying away on the stones.

I wiped my brow and looked round at Cynara, pale and shaking at my back. I had not known she had the weapon or that she knew how to use it!

"They're gone," she said, and I heard the effort she was making to keep her voice steady, "but they may be back. I'll keep watch here, while you're in the Tower."

I nodded, my breath coming in great gasps, and went into the Tower. There might not be much time. If Karamy had set this trap for me, there might be others. I went up the stairs, slowly, rounding every bend with caution, but the Tower was silent and deserted.

Quickly, I ransacked room after room, to no avail. When she took my memories, Karamy had also been careful to take anything that would give me power over any of the Dreamers, even old Rhys. As for the thing that would force Narayan to my will again, I could find it nowhere.

I went up more stairs until I stood at the very pinnacle of the Tower; Adric's star-room; into which I had been catapulted—was it less than three days ago? I stood at the high window, vaguely thinking of a younger self, an Adric who had watched the stars here, not alone. I traced back through the years, diving down into the seas of sudden memory, and brought up the knowledge of—

"Kenscott!" said a voice behind me, and I whirled to look into the face of a man I had never seen before.

He had the primitive look of a man out of the forgotten past. I had seen such creatures as I swam in the nowhere of the Time Ellipse. He was tall, clean-shaven; he looked athletic; his eyes and hair were a ridiculous color, pale brown. He looked angry, if he could be said to have any expression at all.

But he spoke clearly and with deliberate calm.

"Well, Michael Kenscott," he said, "you have taken

my place very nicely. I suppose I should thank you. You've fooled Karamy into giving me my freedom, and Narayan into giving me his trust, and the rest, I think I can manage for myself!" He laughed. "In fact, you're so much *me* that you don't seem to know who you are! What weak creatures you people are! But I *can* force you back into your own body, such as it is."

The man was mad! At any rate, he'd insulted the Lord Adric in his own Tower, and by Zandru's eyelashes, he'd pay for it! I flung myself at him with a yell of rage; my fingers dug into his throat.

And I cried out in the strangling clutch of long lean fingers grabbing at me, clutching my shoulders, biting into my neck.

An agonizing wrench shuddered over my body, a painful and somehow familiar jolt.

I faced—
Adric!

CHAPTER TEN

OF COURSE I understood, even while I fought, dizzy and reeling, to loosen the death-grip I'd put on my own throat. I was back, I was me, I was Mike Kenscott again.

Adric loosened his hands of his own free will, and stepped away, breathing hard. "Thank you," he said, in the harsh voice that had been mine for so long. "I myself could hardly have done better. No, I won't strangle you."

With one swift movement, he snatched something from a little recess in the wall—pointed, twisted—and fired pointblank at me. A white bolt zipped at me.

To my amazement, only a pleasant, tingling heat warmed me. I had enough split-second reasoning reflex left to claw at my breast and fall in a slumped huddle to the ground. Adric fumbled in his pockets, half-drew his sword as if to reassure himself it was there; pulled out the little mirror I had taken from Evarin, still wrapped in its protective silks. I watched, breathless, between narrowed eyelids. If he would only look into it.

Instead, with a shudder of disgust, he flung it at me. With a braced, agonizing effort, I made myself lie perfectly still, not flinching to avoid the blow. The thing struck my forehead; I felt blood break to the surface and trickle wetly down my face. I heard Adric's firm receding steps and the risp of a closing door. He was gone.

I moved. To this day I am not sure how I escaped death from Adric's weapon, but I believe it was because I was in my own body—and *his* world. After I had touched Adric the first time, my reaction to earth's electricity had changed. In this world I was not immune to their forces, but I could absorb them without damage. I wiped the blood from my temple, glancing with brief, startled recognition at my own hands again.

Cynara! Cynara, waiting at the foot of the Crimson Tower, waiting for *me,* in Adric's body! I forgot that, overshadowed by Adric's memories, I had plotted against Narayan and Cynara; remembered, with anguish, the trust in Cynara's eyes. *What would Adric do to her and to Narayan?*

I grabbed up the mirror, crammed it into my pocket. Against the nightmare haste that drove me, I ran to the closet I remembered from that first day; quickly, from the racks of weapons, chose a short, ugly knife. I wouldn't need swordsman's training to use that!

Thank God, I knew my way around the place; I could remember everything I had done when I was Adric! But I could also "remember" what he had done when he was me! (A vague, shocking memory of a scene with Andy half-stopped my heart, but I had no time for that now.) That meant that Adric could also "remember" everything that I had done and planned with Narayan!

This crazy, mixed-up business of identity! Would I ever again be sure which of us was which?

I dashed out of the tower room, ran down the endless stairs three at a time, heart pounding. The fallen zombie-guards still lay dead in the courtyard, but there was no sign of Cynara, nor of Adric.

"Cynara!" I shouted her name.

An eerie screaming answered me, and a dangerous whirring of wings suddenly beat around my head. I staggered, almost fell backward as one of the murderous falcons, the one in blue, darted at me. I backed against the wall, but the bird darted in again; I drew my knife, but the bird hung off. Suddenly it made another dart; I edged along the wall, knife poised. Again it veered away and hung there, regarding me with those live eyes. The damned bird was *herding* me toward the blue tower!

And Gamine had not flown falcon with the others! Cautiously, I moved toward the blue tower walls; the falcon followed me at a careful distance, out of knife-reach, hovering. Experimentally I took a step back toward the crimson tower, and the bird darted in again, the strong pinions beating in the enclosed space, the vicious little beak thrusting at me.

Cynara! What had happened to her? I tried to dodge past the bird; was enveloped in the flapping darkness of wings, beating hard against my face. Spent, breathless, I let myself be driven back and back, toward the blue walls of Gamine's tower; retreated slowly up the stairs, step after step.

The bird darted past me, poised in the stair-well. Blindly I slashed upward with the knife, was rewarded with a splatter of thin burning blood, but the bird, still not disabled, darted and pecked at me, driving me up and up.

"All right, damn it," I grated, ducked beneath the

threshing wings and ran, up the stairs toward the pinnacle of the blue tower. Behind me, abruptly, the falcon flapped, threshed, went limp and rolled down the stairs, a tangle of wings, landing far below with a flailing thump, the life withdrawn from it.

I paused on the stairs, breathing hard. What now? Gamine was no friend to Adric, I knew that. My memories of Adric did not help me here; Adric had had a blankness in his memory around Gamine, a blurring and invisibility, a place where sight and memory stopped short. Had he ever seen Gamine?

Could Gamine help me against Adric?

What was Adric doing now? I had served him well; won Narayan's trust, then turned him loose again in his own body, to betray and destroy Narayan again—the one hope against Rainbow City, delivered into the hands of the man who had first freed, then turned against him!

And even yet I could not wholly hate Adric. I had lived three days and three nights in Adric's body and brain; I knew his strengths, his weaknesses, his dreams and his torments, his desires and his fears. I could not wholly condemn him.

He had done good once. He had freed the Dreamer, he had shared Narayan's dream of freeing Narabedla from the slavery of the Rainbow City, but why had he changed? Karamy's devilments? Few men would be to blame for yielding to Karamy's spells, the Golden Witch of Narabedla.

A shadow flitted across my sight; the robed and veiled Gamine stood above me in the stair-well, an air of cold amusement in the Spell-singer's mocking voice. "How like you this body, Adric? You are beaten now for sure! The stranger works with Narayan in your body, Adric!" The cold, neutral laughter chilled my blood. "Watch and see what *you* will do!"

"I'm not Adric," I shouted. "Adric's in his own body again, he got back, he's going to betray Narayan and Cynara."

"I expect you would like me to believe that," Gamine murmured, contempt in the clear, sexless voice.

I clenched my fists, shaking with rage at the delay. Cynara at Adric's mercy, and Narayan. Suddenly I thought of the one person who would know. Rhys!

"Let me by to Rhys," I begged. "He'll know that I'm telling the truth!" *How did I know that?* Gamine laughed, and, infuriated by the mocking laughter, I shouted "Damn you, let me by," and thrust out my arms to move Gamine forcibly out of my way.

Whatever Gamine was—woman, man, imp, witch or robot—it was not human. Steel wires seemed to writhe between my hands. I struggled impotently with that bonebreaking grip; then, on swift impulse, thrust my hands swiftly at the blurred invisibility where Gamine's face should have been.

Gamine screamed, a thin cry of horror and despair. Suddenly I knew where I had been during those two weeks in the hospital when Adric lay lifeless in my body, in the hospital, in my place, crushed and shocked with unfamiliar force. An instinct I had grown to trust warned me to pull away, sharply, from Gamine's relaxed grip. I shouldered by and ran like hell.

Halfway up the last flight of stairs, I heard the Spell-singer's running feet behind me; I quickened my stride and sprinted for the heavy door at the top of the steps. I could *feel* Rhys's presence behind that door! I threw my weight against the door, twisted the handle frantically.

The door was locked.

Behind me I heard the soft, silk-shod feet of Gamine, and hopelessly I put my back to the door, my hand on Adric's knife. *If there was no other way—*

The door opened suddenly and I was flung backward, sprawling, into the room. "Well, Michael Kenscott," said the old, tired voice of Rhys, "you are a fool, but Gamine is no better. I knew you were not strong enough to crowd out Adric, but I had to try. Yes, I knew you were coming. I know where Adric has gone. I know where Narayan is, and what they plan to do."

I picked myself up angrily from the floor. The old Dreamer's calm voice, his serene wrinkled face beneath the peaked cowl, stirred me to sudden blind rage. I clenched my fists and advanced on him. "You know all that? Is there anything you don't know?"

Gamine had come into the room behind me; the old Dreamer stared over my shoulder at Gamine and said wearily, "I don't know whether you can stop them now. I let it go too far because I wanted peace, because I still hoped—" he spread his hands in a curious, hopeless gesture. The dreamy look of the very old, or the very young, was on his face. "I hoped —but no matter. It is time, Gamine. You must go with Narayan to the Dreamer's Keep."

"No," Gamine whispered in protest. "Narayan cannot go there! His talisman was destroyed! When Adric freed him, still fearing him, Adric kept the talisman and Karamy took it from him, and destroyed it!"

So that was what Adric had been seeking, without my knowing why. If I had found the talisman, and put it into Narayan's hands, then indeed the Dreamer would be free; free of the device—my training interpreted it as electronic waves, attuned somehow to the brain of the Dreamers—that would cast him into tranced sleep if he came within the magnetic field. Bearing his talisman to damp out the special electronic vibrations, Narayan could go where he would, even into Rainbow City, or the Dreamer's Keep.

But the talisman had been destroyed. Adric, his memories blurred by Karamy's magic, did not know that. A part of Adric's power over Narayan was gone. At least, Adric could not take and keep the talisman as he had planned, but Narayan was forever barred from freedom and from the full use of his power.

The talisman—magic? A special vibration device that held and concentrated the powers of the mind? I did not know. Maybe "magic" was only another word for a force that I could not understand. But the talisman was the bond between the sleeping Dreamer and the Narabedlan bound to him, through which the Dreamer's mind drew on the energy of the sacrifice, transferred that power to his master.

Old Rhys had lowered his head into his hands. Now he slowly raised his eyes.

"There is still mine. Give it to him, Gamine."

At Gamine's cry of dismay, Rhys' voice was suddenly a whiplash. "Give it to him! I still have power to—to compel that, even from you! What does it matter what happens to me? I am old, Gamine—old, and it is Narayan's turn, and yours!"

Gamine sobbed, harshly. From the silken veils the

Spell-singer drew forth a small jeweled thing. Like Evarin's mirror, it was wrapped in insulating silks. She untwisted the silk.

It was fashioned like a small sword, not a dagger, but a perfectly proportioned sword, a Toy. The hilt was an intricate pattern of blue crystals. It was about eight inches long. Briefly, another memory not mine touched me.

They were always made in the shape of a weapon, these talismans, symbols of the most powerful weapon known to Rainbow City, the power over the Dreamers.

Evarin's make, this Toy; Adric had seen its fashioning, when Gamine had been bound to the old Dreamer—so old that he could safely be freed from the Dreamer's Keep, bound by ties of blood to Narabedla. Gamine had not cared for power. Gamine had chosen only this: to sit at the feet of old Rhys and learn his wisdom. And this had given Rhys the freedom of Rainbow City.

"Michael must take it from your hands," Rhys' voice was gentler. "While you hold it, I am still bound to you, Gamine. The power must be transferred by an act of will. Then, with this in his own hands, Narayan will be free to go where he will, even to the Dreamer's Keep. Give it to Michael, Gamine." Rhys sat down, wearily, as if the effort of talking had tired him past bearing. I stood and listened, with a rebellious patience, but my eyes were on the little Toy in Gamine's hands. It winked blue. It shimmered. It pulsed with a curious heartbeat, half-hypnotic. Rhys watched too, his tired face intent, almost eager.

"Gamine. If Adric had seen you, had remembered—"

"I want him to remember!" Gamine's low wail was a weird keening in the silent room, and Rhys sighed.

"I cannot tell where this will end," he said at last. "I am Narabedlan. I could not destroy my own people. Gamine is not bound, nor you, Michael Kenscott. I suppose I am a traitor, but when I was born, Narabedla was a fair city, without so many crimes on its head. I have lived to see power grown to a vast evil, and I have let it grow. Now there must be an end. Go and warn Narayan."

Gamine hovered near me, intent, jealous, the shrouded gaze fixed on Rhys. The old man said in a fading voice, "Give it to him, Gamine, and let me rest. Stand away from me, Michael. I have made an end. I do not want to be bound again to you."

I did not understand and stood stupidly still; Gamine gave me an angry shove. "Over there, you fool!"

I reeled, recovered my balance; stood where Gamine directed, about twelve feet from the couch where old Rhys leaned back against the cushions, half-reclining. The old man laid one hand on the hilt of the Toy talisman sword in Gamine's fingers.

"My poor city," he whispered. "Alas, for the Children of the Rainbow! Yet once their towers were fair beneath the double sun."

He took his hand away. He lay back on the cushions. Abruptly Gamine thrust the toy sword into my hands. I felt a sudden stinging shock, like electric current, jolt my whole body; saw Gamine's robed form quiver with the same jolt. The Toy in my hand was suddenly heavy, heavy as if made of lead, and the tiny winking in the hilt was dulled, dim, dead.

The peaked hood of Rhys dropped lower; lay unstirring over his face.

Gamine caught my arm roughly, and the steel of those inhuman fingers bit to the bone as they hauled me almost bodily from the room. I heard the echo of a sob in the Spell-singer's whispering croon.

Rhys farewell!

The next thing I knew, we were racing side by side down flight after flight of stairs. Together, we fled through the subterranean passages of Rainbow City. We came out into the pillared court where, two nights before, the Children of the Rainbow had assembled to ride to the Dreamer's Keep.

And across the courtyard I saw the form of a man. His brown tunic was ripped and torn, his pale face smeared with dirt or blood; he moved slowly, struggling, forcing himself as if he moved through quicksand, falling to his knees, sprawling, then painfully dragging himself upright again in a weary crawl. He braced himself with his two hands and stared at me, almost without comprehension, then his dragging hands moved—for a weapon, a spell?

There was no time for explanations. I threw myself at his knees in a tackle no football coach would be proud of, but it did the trick. Narayan went down, sprawling weakly on the flagstones, struggling with the last remnants of strength.

Good God! What sheer will-power, what iron strength, had let him force himself so far into the Rainbow City, into the power of the terrible vibrations which were spell-binding to a Dreamer? His gray eyes, glazed with pain, looked at me with suspicion and helpless hate, and he forced his slow, painful movements upright, to his knees.

"Narayan, listen," I said urgently, seizing his shoulders, feeling the man tense himself against me, "I'm not one of Karamy's men!"

"Cynara, he's got Cynara," the Dreamer muttered dizzily. "Cynara—who in Zandru's hells are you?" He was almost unconscious, holding onto awareness with iron will.

"Michael Kenscott." Suddenly, knowing it was the best way to establish my good faith, I pulled out the Toy Gamine had put into my hand. "I've seen Rhys. He sent you this."

The gray eyes were blurred, half-conscious, but he held out his hand to take the thing from me.

In his hand it came alive. The small jeweled Toy flared suddenly brilliant, dazzled with a wild sunburst of faceted light: blue, golden, crimson, flame-orange, opal. Narayan's pale struggling face eased; the glazed eyes cleared, and he pulled himself up to his feet, erect and strong, alert, drawing a deep breath of relief and release, and letting it go again.

"In my own hands," he murmured, almost disbelieving. "Free! I'm free!" Then, shaking his head and coming out of his half-ecstatic contemplation, he started, and thrust the talisman inside his shirt.

"Michael Kenscott," he said, looking keenly at me. "Yes, I can sense that. I knew, when Adric came, that he had—changed."

"He's got Cynara?" I demanded.

Narayan nodded, grimly, speaking with hard restraint. "Yes. He surprised me, knocked me out. I fought, but he dragged me inside the court, where I was powerless. I felt my strength going. Cynara heard me cry out, and came and he dragged her away."

He looked past me. The robed, cowled figure of Gamine came noiselessly forward; stopped, a pace or two away from Narayan. I tensed, but Narayan's gray eyes only widened, grew grave.

Then:

"Gamine," he said, very softly. "At last, face to face. Gamine."

"Rhys is gone. But I am here, Narayan, and the time has come." Gamine's soft, sweet voice was barely audible.

"The time has come."

CHAPTER ELEVEN

I BROKE IN rudely, thrusting between the Dreamer and the robed form. "You can stand here like that," I accused, "but Adric's got Cynara! What will he do with her?" Cynara, the one real, human thing in this world, the one who had trusted me, who had even pitied and trusted Adric, and Adric had played on her trust, carried her away, God knows where!

Narayan said tensely, "He'll take her to the Dreamer's Keep. It's just the sort of revenge he'd want to try—" his voice strangled.

"How much start had he? Narayan?"

"I don't know. I'm not sure how long I was unconscious. No matter how we ride, we'll be too late." He clenched his fists in helpless rage and pain. "We'd need wings to stop him!"

Gamine cried out, low, "Wings! But we have wings! The falcons, Narayan! Evarin left the birds here!"

Narayan's face was convulsed, but he shook his head, resolutely. "No, Gamine. I can't. If I save Cynara, I lose the only chance to—to destroy the power of Narabedla. I can't take that chance. She—" he choked. "She wouldn't want me to; we've all risked too much to let one life stand in our way." He turned, grimly. "Come on! We'll ride to the Dreamer's Keep."

But Gamine caught at me, with that strange strength. "You, Michael," she said. "You can stop Adric, or delay him! You can go on the wings of a falcon!"

"What?"

And abruptly the memory rushed over me. The weird half-memory I had thought a dream. Adric, half-dazed, not knowing whether he was himself or some other, come back from the Time Ellipse, Mike Kenscott only a dazed atom in his mind; Adric, his memory gone but knowing by instinct that he had to warn Narayan, and knowing no other way. He had stolen into the room of the falcons, he had taken over the bird, he had flown—

Narayan was blinking at me, wide-eyed. "We saw a falcon," he said, low. "We thought it was one of Evarin's spies, and Raif shot it. So Adric really did try to warn me, once, before Karamy got him into her power again." He looked grieved, unhappy, but he turned to me. "Michael, Gamine is right. We are needed in the Dreamer's Keep, Gamine and I, but you —you can overtake Adric, and delay him, at least. Go as a falcon!"

A flood of ice-water seemed to drench my being. That was crazy, impossible, a weird dream! And I'd just gotten back into my own body, after all this time, and I damned well wasn't going to get out of it again! I tried to explain all this to Narayan, but he only repeated, his face drawn and troubled, "It's Cynara's only chance. Michael, I've no right to ask you, you don't owe us anything. But for Cynara—"

For Cynara. Cynara, who had trusted me, who had known I wasn't Adric, who had, perhaps, saved me in Narayan's camp. The thought turned my blood cold, but I held myself together with both hands, and said thickly, "All right. I'll try. What—what do I have to do?"

Narayan gripped my hand, painfully hard. "Good," he muttered. "Show him, Gamine!"

"Quick! This way!"

I followed the robed form along a passageway, hauntingly familiar, dreamishly strange. A curious, sick, almost exhilarating fear braced every muscle in my body with tingling force, as a dark door opened and I saw the limp shapes of my dream.

Moving slowly, hesitantly, searching with every move for the right feel (to match the vague and elusive memory of a dream?) I reached up and pulled down one of the limp feather-shapes. It was a fluffy crimson mass, and felt curiously warm to the touch, not the cool neutral feel of cloth or feathers. Gamine stood by, not interfering. But when I held it between my hands I turned to the robed and enigmatic form, suddenly not sure.

"What do I do now? Adric had some sort of way to transfer his mind, his consciousness." I stood staring down at the feather-thing, like a limp pillow, in my hands. "I don't."

Gamine said, very low, "Pull it over your head. Like a cloak."

I started to unfold the thing; stopped, shaking, at a razor-touch that left a thin line of blood on my hands. Talons! I stared at the fine-steel claws, so exquisitely shaped, but Gamine made an impatient sound and I pulled it carelessly about my shoulders.

Almost immediately I felt the strange, not unpleasant sensation I remembered, as if my head were expanding like a great gaseous balloon, as if

I were soaring up into the ceiling. I felt the falcon-wings expanding, beating—

Dimly I heard Gamine's warning cry, but the exhilaration of flight was already on me; with a great extending of wings, I fluttered, was flying. My eyesight was suddenly sharper, from a new perspective, the room forming strange new prisoning outlines around me. Not caring, I saw a clumsy two-legged body slump nerveless to the floor, saw an indistinct form fling the window wide, and I was out and gone on the buffeting winds, mounting higher and higher in a sort of ecstasy of soaring flight. . . .

The sky was colorless pale, but not empty space. With strange new perceptions I could see, like layered ribbon, the currents of the wind and air. I rode them upward, dipped one wing and transferred to a shimmering downcraft, playing, intoxicated with the sense of space and freedom.

All my life I had been earthbound! Now for the first time I had the freedom of a dream, to lift and soar, float motionless on a scrap of wind, then with a mere touch of motion, drift and hover like a skimming cloud. . . .

Far, far below me, the rainbow towers were sharp-edged and bright, toylike. Thick, dark carpet of forest dimmed the curve of the land below me, and far away, low on the horizon, a dark-rising shape—

The Dreamer's Keep! The sight recalled me to myself, brought me back from the intoxicating forgetfulness; Adric bore Cynara into danger, while I played here on the wings of the wind, carefree as a bird. . . .

Quickly, I took stock and oriented myself. I was hovering at a great height above the Rainbow City;

far, far below I saw the court and the gate, and three tiny figures that might have been mounted men, racing along the roadway. That was not what I wanted. I spread my wings, riding a swift pale perceptible current of air, and sped eastward.

Tonight the forest was deserted, though I made out, with the supernaturally-keen eyes of the falcon, the small moving shapes of pale deer and other strange animals. But nothing human moved in the forests tonight. Narayan's men had all been drawn away on a grave errand.

I soared up and up to a still greater height. The land was still clear and sharp-edged beneath me, every outline distinct—the sort of vision you get from a tremendously good pair of night glasses. Far away on the horizon I saw a great moving mass of men; Narayan's army on the march? Further still, serried ranks moving grimly, I caught a glimmer of red and gold and knew that Karamy's army of the living dead were prepared to meet the attack. But what of Karamy, Evarin, Idris? Was their deadly cavalcade already at the Dreamer's Keep, was the awful sacrifice already on its way to doom? I didn't know what Narayan's powers might be, now that he was freed, but could he alone, whatever his psi force, dare to face three Narabedlans newly charged with force from that deadly sacrifice? Karamy, Idris, Evarin would be filled to the brim with power from their Dreamers—in their tranced sleep, glutted with life-energy, giving it up to the Narabedlans.

And Adric was racing to join them—and he had Cynara! But where, where?

Grateful for the telescope sight of the falcon, I quartered the country inch by inch, tracing the roads that wound like white ribbons through the forest. Adric would take the shortest and straightest road.

There, *there!* Far below me, a solitary horseman raced, crouched over the neck of his steed, a limp, dark burden across his saddle. Adric!

I heard my own curses like a high shrill falcon-cry, and forced it back to silence. That cry might have warned him! Wheeling, soaring, I rode the downdraft in a long spiral, centering in on that solitary horseman. Silent, tipping my wings, I soared in, and strange, non-human calculations flickered curiously through my mind; I was aware of his body as juicy warmth, conscious of the motion of his horse as a tensile interplay of muscle against air, and the bare back of his neck was like a white glimmering magnet. Strike there, strike *there!* I hung motionless on the wind above him, beating my pinions just enough to match the speed of his horse, centering in on that vlunerable patch of skin where I could thrust, take purchase on his broad shoulders, strike at the root of the brain.

But I waited too long. Perhaps some small rustle of wings, perhaps the bird-shadow crossed his sight, but Adric jerked his body upright in the saddle, arching his back, crying out curses. He was warned! Cautiously I hung off, watching; then darted in, going for his eyes.

But his reflexes were lightning-fast, and he was an old hand at this game. The slapping edge of a weighted cloak struck one wing, knocking me off balance; I had to beat both wings to keep from falling like a stone, and when I balanced again on the air, he had his sword out and was sweeping it in those great arcs I remembered.

I flapped my wings in fury, beating back on the air. I could not reach him without being cut to ribbons! I circled him, grimly, seeking an opening.

Across the saddle Cynara stirred and moaned. Adric cursed, his glance going swiftly from the girl to my hovering beak above him, and I exulted; *now if Cynara can use her head, she can divide his attention just enough* ...

Adric's sword-room was lessened with the girl stirring; he could not move freely, and I dived in, hearing Cynara's scream of terror. I struck between Adric and the girl, clawing, darting in my beak, wings beating. Adric toppled backward, overbalanced; the horse reared, and Cynara slid to the ground, struck heavily and lay still. I darted in, ready to strike, but Adric recovered, and had his sword out, making a steel ring between himself and me.

I cursed and heard again the eerie falcon-scream of rage and frustration, hanging away again. I circled behind him, but he turned, warily, keeping guarded. I darted into a sudden opening; slashed, was rewarded with an explosion of curses from Adric, and saw a long gash slowly open in his forearm; but he recovered swiftly, swung his sword up and I overbalanced, tipped, feeling the flight-feather gone from one wing. Strangely, I felt no pain, but a spasm of panic fear. I had to struggle for balance.

I saw Cynara raise herself, slowly, to a sitting position. Her eyes were wide with terror. I circled in again, feeling the crippling weight in my wounded wing. Now I must risk all! I dived in like an airplane, zooming straight at Adric's face. I took him off guard and he overbalanced, fell backward; my claws slashed blood from his cheek as I dug my talons into him, wings beating, gripping for balance. I bent my beak for the kill.

His left arm sliced upward; with an eerie scream of fury I saw—too late!—the sharp-pointed dagger in his hand. I felt it slice through one wing; plunge into my heart. I saw a splatter of burning yellow venom, heard Cynara's scream, and I was. ...

... I was clinging, sick and shaking, to the saddle of a galloping horse. Rising wind beat in my face; above me the moons swung in an indigo sky, and sparks beat from the horse's hoofs on frosty stone. I gasped, for a moment disoriented, wobbling dangerously, not knowing what had happened.

Then awareness came. I had lost. Adric had killed the falcon, and I was back in my own body. ...

Riding! Narayan's blonde hair was frosty pale in the moonlight; he rode at my side, straight in the saddle, his face drawn and intent. At my other side, the robed Gamine was a nightmare ghost, a phantom.

"Narayan!" I gasped.

He turned in his saddle; drew his horse up for a moment.

"You're back! What happened? Adric—"

"I failed," I said bitterly, and told them. Narayan looked grim, but his hand gripped my shoulder. "Easy! You did the best you could, and at least you may have delayed him enough."

"But how did I get here?"

"We brought you with us," Gamine said sharply. "Enough talking! Ride!"

It took all my concentration to stick on the animal's back, but I was acquiring balance and a feel for riding. *The ill wind was blowing some good,* I thought inanely.

Far away we heard the sudden spatter of gunfire, the screams of dying men, the ring of swords and spears, the shrill cry of a falcon. Narayan's face looked haunted.

"Kerrel and his men have met the guards! They're attacking!"

The scream of falcons rang swiftly over Gamine's head. The too-familiar beat of wings slapped over my back; I flung up one arm to knock away one serpentine neck. My terrified horse plunged and bucked, and I rocked in the saddle, nearly falling. Another bird swooped down on Narayan, and another, and then there were swarms of them, gold and purple and green, crimson, blue, flame-color; the air was thick with their wings. Gamine screamed. I saw Narayan beating the air with his sword; the veiled Spell-singer, crouching in the saddle, was lashing them with a whip. The lash kept the birds at bay, but the razor claws caught at the blue shroudings.

Narayan, whip in one hand, sword in the other, beat round him in great arcs, and I heard one bird's death-cry send ringing echoes through the forest. I got my knife out, slashed upward.

"The mirror," screamed Gamine, "Evarin's mirror! Quick, they're coming by millions!"

They were, indeed, coming in scores, darkening the sky; whirling and screeching, an army of ghastly death. These were not the soul-falcons such as I had flown, elaborately endowed with the intelligence of their launcher and all his human cunning; these were machines. Alive, yes, and deadly, but not with the life we know. Only the nightmare freak of a science gone mad could control, or produce, these hateful things that were filling the clean air, groping for us with needle beaks and talons, wild wings beating. Only Evarin—

I fumbled blindly for the mirror-thing, clumsily stripping away the silks around it. A needle-talon raked my wrist, and by sheer instinct I struck upward, turning the face of the mirror toward the bird.

The falcon reeled in mid-air, flapped, went limp and fell. A tingling shock rattled through my arm. I dropped the mirror and leaped to catch it. The thing was a perfect conductor. It drained energy! Now I knew why Evarin had been so anxious to have me— or Adric—gazing into its depths!

The birds were brainless, all pure energy, unless controlled by the personality of the owner, and the Narabedlans had no time for that today, no leisure to play the falcon-game! But Evarin had loosed them against us, in a last desperate play.

I grabbed the mirror, and held it upright; I caught a half-glimpse, from the tail of my eye, of the weird lightnings that coiled inside it, but even that glimpse twisted my stomach in nervous knots. Shielding my face, I held the thing upward. The birds flew toward it like moths streaming around a candle; shock after shock flowed along my arm. Three more of the horrible falcons fell limp, lifeless, drained!

A strange exhilaration began to buoy me up. The force from the birds was not electricity, but some kindred energy which my nerves drank greedily. I thrust the mirror out; was rewarded again with the surge of power, and again the birds, by dozens this time, flapped and fell.

Then, as if whatever had loosed the army of falcons

had realized their uselessness, the whole remaining force of the birds wheeled and fled, winging swiftly overland to the distant donjon that rose high on the horizon.

Recalled to the Dreamer's Keep!

CHAPTER TWELVE

THE FLOW OF strength had renewed me; I felt I could face whatever came. I thrust Evarin's mirror into a packet; flung a word to Narayan and we were riding again, Gamine racing behind us. The blue, shroudlike veils had been slashed to ribbons; I could see the pale gleam of naked flesh through the torn veiling.

The noise of battle behind us grew more distinct; I could make out separate explosions, flashes of colored flame. I shuddered; even now that frightful army of falcons might be winging to join Evarin. The rebels could kill some of them, but for every falcon dead there would be twenty more slaves for Narabedla. What could Narayan's men, with their scythes and pitchforks, do against the incredible science of a Toymaker?

Narayan's strained face was ghastly in the moonlight. I needed no telepathy to read his thoughts. Slaughter for his men. What for his sister? Our horses seemed to lag, to drag through a mire of motionlessness, though they were at the full gallop of endurance.

The sounds of battle drew nearer. Everything in me cried out that I was a fool, riding full tilt into a battle in which I had no personal stake, in a world that was not my own. Yet something else told me, coldly and with a grim truth, that all I possessed was what I might win today, for this was the only world I would ever know, that I would never see my own world again.

Never! And Adric should rot in a hell of his own choosing, for that!

But we were passing the sounds of battle! If we had raced before, now our horses seemed to fly. Behind us the fight raged, men screamed in the agony of death, wounded horses neighed and I heard the muffled sound of earth flying upward, exploding in fire. But the sounds grew dimmer; faded away.

We had left the forest, and were riding across a dark and hummocky plain. Moss padded our hoof-noises; now and then some small furry thing skittered across the track, and twice my horse shied at swooping night-birds and my heart stopped until I saw they were not the falcons of Evarin.

Stark and black now against a treeless horizon I could see the Dreamer's Keep. I rode hunched in the saddle, my eyes on the vast cairn only a few miles away now.

Suddenly a vast arch of lightning spanned the sky above the Dreamer's Keep. Blue lightning. I heard Narayan groan like a man in his death-agony; twisting in my saddle, I saw brooding horror on his face, mingled with pain, and a terrified satisfaction.

"The sacrifice, I still feel it," he breathed, in labored gasps, "I still—take strength from it—Michael!" His voice held unbearable torture, and the veins in the fair face stood out, black and congested with effort. "If I start to—to work for *them*—promise to—promise to shoot me."

"Oh, God—" I gasped.

"Michael, promise! Gamine!"

Gamine spurred her horse to his side; I heard the low, neutral voice, sweet, almost crooning. Again the vast arc of blueness spanned the sky; Narayan dug his spurs into his horse's flank and raced ahead of us.

On the plain, limned starkly in silhouette against the sky, a horseman appeared. He rode low in the saddle, his horse limping, a darkness across his saddle. I cursed; I knew that lean crouched figure, knew it as well as my own! I *had* delayed Adric, but now he rode to the sacrifice, and before him, limp across his saddle, he bore Cynara!

The rest of that nightmare ride is a blank in my memory. The next thing I remember clearly is reining up beneath the lee of the gaunt pile of rocks-on-rocks that was the Dreamer's Keep. There was no sign of Adric, or of Cynara, no sign of any living person, nothing but the incandescent lightning that rayed out every four seconds or so. Narayan's face was a white death-mask, and Gamine's breathing came in short sobs. I alone was free of the effect; my body throbbed and tingled with the weird energy set free in the night.

We flung ourselves from our horses. Gamine tugged futilely at the torn veils, and for the first time the blurred invisibility wavered and I caught a glimpse of one blue eye, blue as the sky-lightnings that rose and flamed and died.

The tower dwarfed us with its massive bulk, rising sheer for hundreds of feet. Gamine clutched my arm. "Listen!"

All I could hear was a low, not unpleasant humming, like the singing drone of great bees, or high-tension wires, but the sound struck them with horror. Narayan fumbled in his shirt; drew forth the little talisman Rhys had given me, and at the sight of it his haggard face relaxed. He gripped it tightly in his hands; drew a long moaning sigh, closed his eyes for a moment.

Somewhere above us a shivering scream rang out. It broke the static immobility that held us; Narayan, slipping the Toy inside his shirt again, began to run around the Keep, Gamine and I panting at his heels. We came around the corner beneath an arching outcrop of stonework. No one needed to give orders; as one, we scrambled up on the ledge, crowding close together. I gripped my hand on the knife in my belt; it had a comforting solid feel. I needed that.

A framed archway let us look down into the interior of the Keep. Below us a voice cried out in despair and unbelief. "Adric, Adric! No, oh no!"

The voice was Cynara's.

Under our combined weight the glass shattered; we hurled inward. We found ourselves standing on a great shelf, about ten feet above the floor of the Keep, looking down at a scene framed in stark horror. Golden Karamy, dwarfed Idris, Evarin, stood in a close circle about a ring of coffins that glowed pale crystal, gleamed with scintillant radiance. In the hand of each of the Narabedlans was a tiny, jewelled sword, a Toy, and in the coffins—

Gamine screamed. "The Dreamers!"

Not till then did we see what Adric was doing. At the center of the ring of coffins, a dais rose upright, horribly altar-like, and a line of the mindless slaves, nude, vacant-eyed, moved in single file before that dais. As each one stepped forward, there was a shuddering moan, the tiny swords glared with light, and the slave—was not!

And Adric, Cynara captive between his hands, was thrusting her forward, into the space between the coffins, toward the nexus of blue light, toward the Sacrifice-stone of the Dreamers!

The sight put me beyond caution. We threw ourselves from the ledge, and went down into a writhing, sprawling mass of living flesh. A barked command from Idris, and the slaves swarmed on us, drowning us in smothering bodies. I kicked and sprawled and thrashed and scratched and bit my way to the top of the heap, and somehow, for a second, I rolled free.

That instant was enough. I was on my feet, the knife in my hand. Dragging bodies clung at my heels; I kicked out savagely, felt my boot strike naked flesh, felt and heard the pulpy sound of a skull crushing under the impact of my heel. The sound rocked my stomach, but I was not in a position to be fastidious. My eyes were swimming in trickling blood. Gamine clawed free, and together we elbowed out of the press.

Evarin sprang at me. I thrust blindly with the knife in my hand, ripped into his shoulder, missing the throat by inches. I caught the talisman Toy from his hand as it fell free. A moment of the clinging, tearing melee; then Gamine and Narayan and I were standing back to back in the center of the ring of coffins. There was a long howl of pain and terror from Evarin and the four Narabedlans flung themselves backward in terror.

For within the coffins there was a stirring....

But Adric was no coward. He threw himself backward, grasped Cynara again and with all the force of his lean arms he flung the girl straight toward the nexus of blue light! Narayan and Gamine stood frozen, but I broke free, dashed forward, I passed straight across the cone of blue lightning—

Unharmed!

The blasting energy only tingled pleasantly in my body as I caught Cynara in mid-air and reeled away from the force that would have meant utter annihilation for her. Narayan caught Cynara's staggering body from my arms, drew her back to safety. Then I felt the impact as Adric's tall, heavy body crashed against me, felt the shock as my fist smashed into his jaw, and heard him grunt as we locked into a clinch that carried us nearer, and nearer to that center of blue energy! A moment we swayed there, at the very edge of the lightnings.

Then Evarin's tensed cat-body lit into the center of my back.

Again the heat thrust needles through me. Adric was flung clear, but there was an arch of blue that spanned the vault, a wild scream like the death-cry of a panther—

The Toymaker was gone!

Within the coffins the blue lights flared, as if the last shock of energy had freed them. Quickly Idris and Karamy ran forward, thrusting the talisman Toys against the very lids of the coffins, but too late. The Toys in the hands of Narayan and Gamine spat glaring blue fire, and step by step the Narabedlans retreated, farther, farther, farther. . . .

The coffins were suddenly empty. As if by magic, three men and a woman clustered around Narayan and Gamine. In their faces I could distinguish a curious likeness to Narayan, and to old Rhys; and Narayan, within the circle of Dreamers, reached out and flung the tattered veils from Gamine. A triumphant chant rushed sweetly from the lips of the Spellsinger as the veils came away and at the center of the mutants stood Gamine the Dreamer, dwarfing them all with her majesty, a Dreamer who had never slept, never been bound. She was a woman, as I had begun to guess, slender and fair and very beautiful, and I thought of Isis and the young Osiris as her blue eyes blazed and the lovely body arched upward in tall freedom from the shrouding veils. The blue lightnings swirled and faded, and the Dreamer's Keep was bathed with trembling, glimmering rainbows.

Karamy and Idris retreated, step by slow step, slinking backward into the shadows. Only Adric stood his ground. He looked dazed, his eyes fixed on Gamine, but he did not falter.

The rainbows died. The air was void and empty of energy. The Dreamers stood looking on the crouching Karamy with her hidden face; on the bent, gnarled dwarf, on Cynara kneeling white and radiant with joy, on Adric who stood staring at Gamine like a man released from a spell.

Gamine spoke at last. "Rhys was right; the time had come. The time is here, now. What next?"

The circle of Dreamers turned one to another, but Gamine shook her head, her long pale hair lifting electrically around her face. "No. Why should they die? They are only an old dwarf, a silly fool who could not make up his mind." Her eyes dwelt first on Idris, then on Adric. "And Karamy. They have no power, now we are freed. They had not even power to see me as I was, not entirely. Pity them in their weakness. Now we are freed."

Adric drew himself upright. His slackly-parted lips

set firmly, and he looked at Narayan with a dispassionate, stubborn shrug. Then he turned back to Gamine.

"Kill me, if you like."

But it was Narayan who answered, stepping toward the man in crimson with a strange, choking excitement. "No, Adric. I want you to see what you saw before, to see what sent you away, to see the thing that drove you mad. Gamine, Gamine, show him what he saw then."

Gamine came slowly forward to where Karamy knelt.

"Stand up, witch."

Slowly, Karamy rose to her feet. There was no hope in her eyes, no mercy in Gamine's. The two pairs of eyes, cat-yellow and blue, fought for a moment.

"And was I wrong?" Karamy demanded at last, raising her head, her beautiful face set and cold with pride. "I knew you would destroy us, Gamine, and destroy our world. For that I was willing to fight you to the death, and if it is my death, still. What I have done was what had to be done!"

Gamine smiled, faintly. "And by that you stand or fall or die, Karamy?" She turned to the others. "Karamy is beautiful, is she not?"

I suppose no woman on Earth has ever been, or ever will be, as beautiful as Karamy the golden. She stood there, proud and straight, amber and golden and tiger-tawny, and turned her eyes on Adric, and I saw longing and love break forth in the man's eyes. He gazed and gazed, and Karamy held out her arms, and Adric, bemused, went toward her....

"Hold him," Narayan commanded tersely.

One of the Dreamers made a curious sign with his

left hand, and Adric, arrested, stood gripped in a vice of invisible force.

"This was Karamy's power," said Gamine in her clear ringing voice, "but now see Karamy shorn of the Illusion her Dreamer threw to guard her! See the form of Karamy that she made me wear! *This!*"

She reached out and touched Karamy lightly with the little talisman Toy she held.

There was a gasp of horror from many throats. Karamy—Karamy the golden, the exquisite. There are no words for the *kind* and *type* of change that took place before our eyes. I was sick and retching with horror before the metamorphosis was half complete; Cynara was sobbing softly and piteously; but Adric, frozen, could not look away.

Gamine's laugh—low and sweet, and doubly deadly for its sweetness—reached our ears. "Yet I should be grateful," she murmured, mockingly, "for Karamy's magic kept my true shape hidden. So I am free, Karamy, free and a Dreamer, and you, shall I lend you my veils, sister?" Again, the horrible laugh. "No? Go *forth!*" Her voice was a lashing whip, and with a broken wail, the thing that had been Karamy threw up an arm across the staring sockets and fled away into the night. And we never saw it again. ...

So that was the end of Karamy the Golden, the end.

A little later I found that Adric and I were staring stupidly at one another, puzzled, but without animosity. Cynara came and slipped a protecting arm around Adric and I turned away, embarrassed, for the man was sobbing like a child.

I was amazed and sick with the enormity of all I had seen and done; I shook and shivered with deadly chill. I suppose it was reaction.

"Steady!" Narayan's steely hand on my shoulder kept me once again from making a fool of myself.

"You've done a great deal for us," he said. "I wish we had some way of thanking you, not for myself, for millions of people. Perhaps some day we'll find a way of sending you back to your own world, but with Rhys and Karamy gone—"

Adric, looking subdued and speaking with a curious humility, looked at me over Narayan's shoulder. "There will be a way, some day. It will take time to find it, but some day—"

I knew what they meant. The magic of the Dreamers could not be used again in the old ways, and now their power was an unknown quantity. Adric said, "In the meantime—"

"In the meantime, you seem to be stuck with me," I said, and spontaneously we grinned at each other. I could not hate this man. We had known one another too well. Freed of his enchantments ...

He chuckled. "Rainbow City's big enough for us both."

Narayan looked from Adric to me; then Gamine's intent face was at his elbow. "I'll see to these men," she said. "Narayan, they need you." She motioned to the wakened Dreamers, standing in a dazed circle. "They must be told why they were wakened, and how. There are slaves to be freed, armies—"

Narayan glanced guiltily over his shoulder. "That's so," he acknowledged, gravely; squared his shoulders and went to his people. I watched him go, feeling as if my one friend here had deserted me. But it had to be that way. Narayan was not our kind. He was the sort of man who could remodel a world, but the look he gave Adric and me told us that we should have a share, if we liked, in the rebuilding.

Gamine took my hand, and I left Adric and Cynara with a wistful glance. Cynara was lovely, and very human, and I suppose I had hoped that in some way she would compensate for my enforced stay in this world. But if Adric was himself again, could I hope that?

Gamine and I stood on the steps of the Dreamer's Keep and her voice, soft and wistful, mourned in the darkness. "Old Rhys knew I had been born with Dreamer powers, even before I was bound to him. He knew and kept me close to him, hid me and helped me. One day Adric found out. It changed him; he— we freed Narayan, together. Then Karamy made me what I was, what you saw. It hurt Adric—hurt something deep in him. I could have cured him, in time, but Karamy had him bewitched. She stripped him of power, of memory. Perhaps some day he will remember that I was what I was."

"Gamine! Gamine!" Adric's voice cried from within, and the next moment he rushed forth, caught the Dreamer woman in his arms and his mouth met hers, and she stood swaying in his arms, laughing and crying together. Cynara, following slowly, smiled with gentle satisfaction. Over Adric's shoulder, Gamine's blue eyes met mine. Adric knew.

Cynara's voice was tenderly humorous as we left them together, in the glory of the rising red sun. "Poor Gamine," she said, "and poor Adric. I kept an eye on him, for her sake and Narayan's. I was sorry for them both. Michael, I knew—I knew you were not Adric—"

She was very lovely and very human, Cynara, and I remembered how I had looked into her eyes on our first ride together, and hated being the person Adric was then.

"I, a stranger and afraid, in a world I never made—"

"But you did," Cynara said softly, and I realized I had spoken the words aloud. I looked at Adric, clasped in Gamine's arms, standing in the glow of a new day that was dawning for them. He had found his world.

"But it is your world too," Cynara said, and taking my hand in hers, led me down the steps of the Dreamer's Keep, into the strange sunrise. A shout went up from the men assembled around the tower, waiting. I heard it, drew a deep breath and then put my arm around Cynara, calling to Adric to come and share it with me.

Bestselling SF/Horror

☐ The Labyrinth	Robert Faulcon	£2.50
☐ Night Train	Thomas F. Monteleone	£2.50
☐ Doomflight	Guy N. Smith	£2.50
☐ Malleus Maleficarum	Montague Summers	£4.95
☐ The Devil Rides Out	Dennis Wheatley	£2.95
☐ Cities in Flight	James Blish	£2.95
☐ Stand on Zanzibar	John Brunner	£2.95
☐ 2001 – A Space Odyssey	Arthur C. Clarke	£1.95
☐ Gene Wolfe's Book of Days	Gene Wolfe	£2.25
☐ The Shadow of the Torturer	Gene Wolfe	£2.50
☐ The Blackcollar	Timothy Zahn	£1.95
☐ Speaker for the Dead	Orson Scott Card	£2.95
☐ The War for Eternity	Christopher Rowley	£2.95
☐ Contact	Carl Sagan	£3.50

Prices and other details are liable to change

ARROW BOOKS, BOOKSERVICE BY POST, PO BOX 29, DOUGLAS, ISLE OF MAN, BRITISH ISLES

NAME ....

ADDRESS ....

....

....

Please enclose a cheque or postal order made out to Arrow Books Ltd. for the amount due and allow the following for postage and packing.

U.K. CUSTOMERS: Please allow 22p per book to a maximum of £3.00.

B.F.P.O. & EIRE: Please allow 22p per book to a maximum of £3.00.

OVERSEAS CUSTOMERS: Please allow 22p per book.

Whilst every effort is made to keep prices low it is sometimes necessary to increase cover prices at short notice. Arrow Books reserve the right to show new retail prices on covers which may differ from those previously advertised in the text or elsewhere.

Bestselling Thriller/Suspense

☐ See You Later, Alligator	William F. Buckley	£2.50
☐ Hell is Always Today	Jack Higgins	£1.75
☐ Brought in Dead	Harry Patterson	£1.95
☐ Maxwell's Train	Christopher Hyde	£2.50
☐ Russian Spring	Dennis Jones	£2.50
☐ Nightbloom	Herbert Lieberman	£2.50
☐ Basikasingo	John Matthews	£2.95
☐ The Secret Lovers	Charles McCarry	£2.50
☐ Fletch	Gregory Mcdonald	£1.95
☐ Green Monday	Michael M. Thomas	£2.95
☐ Someone Else's Money	Michael M. Thomas	£2.50
☐ Black Ice	Colin Dunne	£2.50
☐ Blind Run	Brian Freemantle	£2.50
☐ The Proteus Operation	James P. Hogan	£3.50
☐ Miami One Way	Mike Winters	£2.50

Prices and other details are liable to change

ARROW BOOKS, BOOKSERVICE BY POST, PO BOX 29, DOUGLAS, ISLE OF MAN, BRITISH ISLES

NAME ....

ADDRESS ....

....

....

Please enclose a cheque or postal order made out to Arrow Books Ltd. for the amount due and allow the following for postage and packing.

U.K. CUSTOMERS: Please allow 22p per book to a maximum of £3.00.

B.F.P.O. & EIRE: Please allow 22p per book to a maximum of £3.00.

OVERSEAS CUSTOMERS: Please allow 22p per book.

Whilst every effort is made to keep prices low it is sometimes necessary to increase cover prices at short notice. Arrow Books reserve the right to show new retail prices on covers which may differ from those previously advertised in the text or elsewhere.

A Selection of Arrow Bestsellers

☐ Live Flesh	Ruth Rendell	£2.75
☐ Contact	Carl Sagan	£3.50
☐ Yeager	Chuck Yeager	£3.95
☐ The Lilac Bus	Maeve Binchy	£2.50
☐ 500 Mile Walkies	Mark Wallington	£2.50
☐ Staying Off the Beaten Track	Elizabeth Gundrey	£4.95
☐ A Better World Than This	Marie Joseph	£2.95
☐ No Enemy But Time	Evelyn Anthony	£2.95
☐ Rates of Exchange	Malcolm Bradbury	£3.50
☐ For My Brother's Sins	Sheelagh Kelly	£3.50
☐ Carrott Roots	Jasper Carrott	£3.50
☐ Colours Aloft	Alexander Kent	£2.95
☐ Blind Run	Brian Freemantle	£2.50
☐ The Stationmaster's Daughter	Pamela Oldfield	£2.95
☐ Speaker for the Dead	Orson Scott Card	£2.95
☐ Football is a Funny Game	Ian St John and Jimmy Greaves	£3.95
☐ Crowned in a Far Country	Princess Michael of Kent	£4.95

Prices and other details are liable to change

ARROW BOOKS, BOOKSERVICE BY POST, PO BOX 29, DOUGLAS, ISLE OF MAN, BRITISH ISLES

NAME ....

ADDRESS ....

....

....

Please enclose a cheque or postal order made out to Arrow Books Ltd. for the amount due and allow the following for postage and packing.

U.K. CUSTOMERS: Please allow 22p per book to a maximum of £3.00.

B.F.P.O. & EIRE: Please allow 22p per book to a maximum of £3.00.

OVERSEAS CUSTOMERS: Please allow 22p per book.

Whilst every effort is made to keep prices low it is sometimes necessary to increase cover prices at short notice. Arrow Books reserve the right to show new retail prices on covers which may differ from those previously advertised in the text or elsewhere.

Bestselling Fiction

☐ Hiroshima Joe	Martin Booth	£2.95
☐ Voices on the Wind	Evelyn Anthony	£2.50
☐ The Pianoplayers	Anthony Burgess	£2.50
☐ Prizzi's Honour	Richard Condon	£2.95
☐ Queen's Play	Dorothy Dunnett	£3.50
☐ Duncton Wood	William Horwood	£3.50
☐ In Gallant Company	Alexander Kent	£2.50
☐ The Fast Men	Tom McNab	£2.95
☐ A Ship With No Name	Christopher Nicole	£2.95
☐ Contact	Carl Sagan	£3.50
☐ Uncle Mort's North Country	Peter Tinniswood	£2.50
☐ Fletch	Gregory Mcdonald	£1.95
☐ A Better World Than This	Marie Joseph	£2.95
☐ The Lilac Bus	Maeve Binchy	£2.50
☐ The Gooding Girl	Pamela Oldfield	£2.95

Prices and other details are liable to change

ARROW BOOKS, BOOKSERVICE BY POST, PO BOX 29, DOUGLAS, ISLE OF MAN, BRITISH ISLES

NAME ....

ADDRESS ....

....

....

Please enclose a cheque or postal order made out to Arrow Books Ltd. for the amount due and allow the following for postage and packing.

U.K. CUSTOMERS: Please allow 22p per book to a maximum of £3.00.

B.F.P.O. & EIRE: Please allow 22p per book to a maximum of £3.00.

OVERSEAS CUSTOMERS: Please allow 22p per book.

Whilst every effort is made to keep prices low it is sometimes necessary to increase cover prices at short notice. Arrow Books reserve the right to show new retail prices on covers which may differ from those previously advertised in the text or elsewhere.